CROSS KNIFE RANCH

Center Point
Large Print

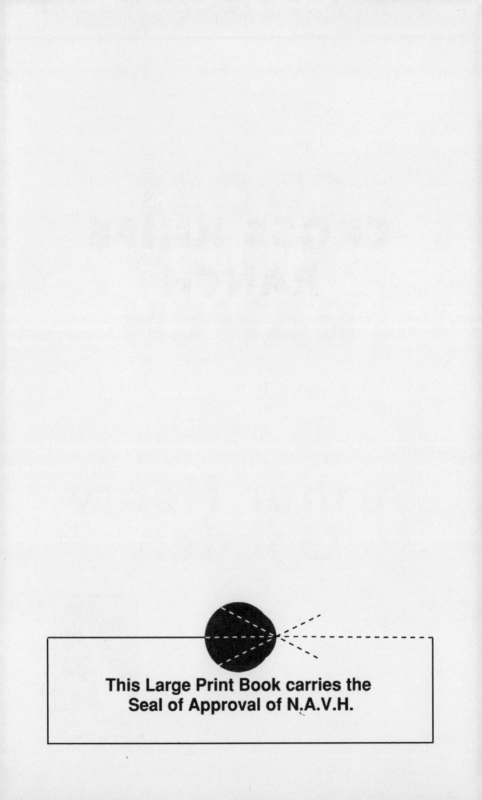

**This Large Print Book carries the
Seal of Approval of N.A.V.H.**

CROSS KNIFE RANCH

Arthur Henry Gooden

CENTER POINT LARGE PRINT
THORNDIKE, MAINE

This Center Point Large Print edition is published in the year 2014 by arrangement with Golden West Literary Agency.

The text of this Large Print edition is unabridged.
In other aspects, this book may vary
from the original edition.
Printed in the United States of America
on permanent paper.
Set in 16-point Times New Roman type.

ISBN: 978-1-62899-088-1

Library of Congress Cataloging-in-Publication Data

Gooden, Arthur Henry, 1879–1971.
Cross knife ranch / Arthur Henry Gooden. —
   Center Point Large Print edition.
pages ; cm
ISBN 978-1-62899-088-1 (librarybinding : alk. paper)
1. Large type books. I. Title.
PS3513.O4767C76 2014
813′.52—dc23
                                        2014000472

CROSS KNIFE RANCH

Chapter I

The man held his horse to a swift running walk through the stunted willows of a dry wash thrusting across the desert towards parched brown hills. The creak of saddle leathers, the grind of shod hoofs against coarse sand, alone disturbed the silence of the brooding wilderness.

There was a youthful buoyancy in the lean hard-muscled body of the rider—an untiring cheeriness reflected in the rangy bay stallion's occasional prancing step. The man may have been thirty, with a certain sun-and-wind bitten maturity in the keen face—a steadiness of alert gray eyes that bespoke cool efficiency. His hair was darkly red—almost black—and Indian straight, and there was a hint of Indian in the rising cheekbones—the high nose. Desert dust streaked tanned face and dark blue shirt, and dulled the silver conchas decorating worn leather chaps. He wore an old black Stetson, pulled over his eyes, and low boots of soft embossed leather, with high heels and spurs. Bearing and dress—the two guns in his holster—marked him with the unmistakable brand of the west. He rode with the tireless ease of his kind, shadowed eyes wary as the dry wash narrowed into a boulder-strewn chasm that twisted up through a shouldering ridge.

Dun-colored streamers of dust hovered above the winding course of the defile, thinning to a pale golden haze against the hot horizon. The stallion raised his head, ears pricking forward, and the man's less acute ears now sensed a low, monotonous murmuring—like the grumbling undertones of distant seas beating upon the shore. He knew the sound for the bawling of cattle—the muffled thud of countless hooves churning the dust that drifted in their wake. A trail-herd—a big one—judging from the rumbling thunder of its approach, was moving toward him through the pass.

He rolled a cigarette, squinting thoughtfully at the warning yellow streamers lifting above the brown hills. The mouth of the pass was wide, running between gentle slopes. He could wait here for the slow-moving herd—or proceed on his way and risk meeting a living wall of tossing horns in the depths of a narrow gorge. With a shrug he shook the stallion to a swinging trot.

The frowning walls closed on them, shutting out the hard glare of the sun, now midway down the western slope. The hovering dust drew closer, with a swelling diapason of bawling cattle. He could hear the shrill urging cries of cowboys, and once, the unmistakable report of a rifle, echoing up the gorge. He looked to his own guns, easing the black butts in the leather holsters, testing their readiness to leap to the flowing swoop of hands.

He rode on steadily, watchful expectancy in the gaze he fixed on each succeeding bend of the trail. His manner indicated a certain sureness of events near at hand, and as a lone rider swung into the turn, he halted the stallion and coolly awaited the other man's approach.

Glimpsing the motionless horseman, the newcomer uttered a shrill yell and sank in spurs.

He came up fast, jerking his gray horse to a plunging halt across the trail.

"Cain't yuh see there's cattle drivin' through, feller? Want to pile 'em up on us?" There was belligerence in the cowboy's voice, suspicion in his cold, unwinking eyes.

"Thought maybe there was a turn-out somewhere," said the stallion's rider mildly.

"No chance," declared the cowboy positively. His cold glance flickered over the big bay horse. "Maybe yore bronc kin run good—but he cain't climb cliffs like no cat, mister."

The other man grinned good-naturedly. "Reckon not, cowboy," he agreed. "Just another of them things that prove it don't pay to go buckin' your own judgment." He swung the stallion round. "Looks like we back-trail a piece."

They rode at a jog trot. Behind them, the narrow gorge suddenly bristled countless tossing horns as the great herd swept clamorously into the turn—surging between the high cliffs—wave upon pressing wave of massed white heads,

9

crowding like foam-breasted seas through the murk.

"Right smart bunch of baldfaces," commented the stallion's rider. "What's your outfit, cowboy?"

The man gave him a sly glance from small beady eyes. "Cain't yuh read brands, mister?" he said ungraciously. He was a stocky, swart person, with a black bristle of unshaven beard, and thin, sneering lips. Two guns sagged in his holster, and thrust under the saddle flap was a rifle. The horse he sat was a superb animal, with lines indicating speed and stamina. "Got eyes, ain't yuh?" He gave his questioner a sour glance.

"Got eyes—and can read brands with 'em," drawled the latter. "Only trouble is, I ain't had a look at the marks on these here dogies." He shrugged indifferently. "Wasn't aimin' to pry into your business."

"See that yuh don't," grunted the cowboy acidly.

"Sure are one friendly hombre, ain't you?" grinned the stranger. "Friendly—like a porcupine." His voice grew sarcastic. "Reckon I'll be relieving you of my poor company by ridin' ahead and waiting outside 'til you and your outfit get through monopolizing this here highway exclusively." He shook his reins and the stallion's stride lengthened.

"Not so fast, mister." There was a snarl in the cowboy's voice—a gun in his hand.

The man in front stared back with a quick jerk

of head, his expression inexpressibly shocked—almost ludicrous with dumb bewilderment.

There was sneering laughter in the cowboy's black eyes. "I'm takin' them guns, mister. Reach for the sky—an' no foolin'."

The stallion's rider obeyed, a dark flush staining the weathered brown of his hawk's face. The cowboy spurred alongside—deftly plucked the black-handled six-shooters from their holsters.

"Now yuh kin ride like yuh want, mister," he said; "only yuh ride just so far ahaid," he added pointedly, "as this hawg-laig o' mine throws hot lead." He thrust the confiscated weapons in his belt.

They rode on wordlessly in the order decreed, while behind them—like a slow-moving flood-tide, followed the massed tossing horns, bearing aloft the far-flung yellow banner of a great trail-herd's march.

They reached the chaparral slopes where the pass made its final thrust between the shouldering cliff, to the sands of the dry wash that sprawled leperously through mesquite and cactus toward the Mexican horizon—a horizon of blinding molten brass, splashed with charcoal shadows that were the distant Sierra Madres.

"We're waitin' here," announced the cowboy as the horses clattered into the pass.

His prisoner reined the bay stallion and stared back at the bellowing herd pouring from the gorge into the bowl-like depression. "Good place to hold 'em," he observed shrewdly. "Could jam in six thousand head and hold 'em 'til hell froze, with one man back in the cut—and another hombre here in the gap." He grinned knowingly. "Right smart place to work over brands—and sure handy—with Mexico lyin' just across the way."

"Yeah?" The cowboy's voice was harsh: "Got it all figgered out, huh?"

"Just a habit of mine—addin' up two an' two," drawled his prisoner. "Not meanin' I aim to poke into your business—"

"Mister," said the cowboy softly, his eyes bleak, "you've said a mouthful. Yuh sure ain't goin' to poke into my business." His gun menaced the other. "Climb outer that saddle, feller."

He loosened his rope as the other obeyed. "Belly up to that cliff," he told him. He climbed from his own saddle and in a few moments had his prisoner securely bound. "Speakin' of brands," he sneered, "there's no call to let yuh strain yore eyes readin' 'em today." He drew his victim's own bandanna over his eyes and knotted the ends.

"Friendly and trustin' by nature, ain't you?" grumbled the blindfolded man, easing against the cliff.

"Just bein' careful," rejoined the cowboy sourly. "Yuh may be all hunky dory—but I'm leavin' it for the boss to figger yuh out."

For nearly an hour the slow movement of cattle

into the little amphitheatre continued. The shrill, urging cries of the cowboys pushing the laggards drew nearer, and presently above the bedlam of bawling cows came the clatter of shod hoofs as the men rode into the gap. The sudden hush of voices as the riders drew rein told the listening prisoner that his person was the object of their silent scrutiny. A snarling voice broke the silence.

"What's goin' on here, Smoky? Who's this jasper?"

"Snagged him back in the pass a ways," explained the cowboy. He laughed thinly. "Figgered you'd like to look the maverick over, Stenger."

There followed another silence, the blindfolded one leaning indifferently against the cliff, seemingly unconcerned at his predicament.

"Sure would like a smoke," he finally announced. "Light me a cigarette—one of you hombres."

The cowboy, Smoky, laughed again. "What yuh make of the buzzard, Stenger?" His voice was complaining. "That's what got my goat—his sorta cool way of talkin'—like he's coverin' up—or just don't give a damn—"

"Coverin' up, huh?"

Stenger climbed from his saddle and went deliberately to the prisoner.

"What's yore name, feller?" he demanded.

"I asked polite-like for a cigarette," murmured the captive reproachfully.

The man, Stenger, scowled. He was a tall, bulky person, with bristly red hair and pale blue angry eyes.

"An' I'm askin' yore name," he growled. "Talk up, stranger!"

"What name would you fancy—Mister—Mister Stenger. I'm always wishful to please—"

Stenger's oath interrupted the mocking voice.

"Who told yuh my name's Stenger?"

"I've ears that hear—even if my eyes can't see," reminded the prisoner. "I could swear that our cautious friend, Smoky, addressed you as Stenger a few moments ago."

There was a laugh from the listening group of riders. Stenger lifted a ham-like hand.

"I've a mind to bust yuh!"

"Nothing to stop you, Mister Stenger," admitted the prisoner in a resigned voice. The teeth under the blinding folds of the bandanna glimmered in a brief smile. "You don't sound like that sort of coward, though."

Stenger grunted furiously, but the knotted knuckles uncurled into exploring fingers that quickly went through his tormentor's pockets.

"Now, Mister Stenger—don't tell me that you're just a cheap pocket thief! You wouldn't take my nineteen dollars and seven cents—would you, Mister Stenger? And my cigarettes and sundry— oh, please—Mister Stenger—"

"Shut yore trap!" shouted the baited cowman.

14

"I'm tryin' to find somethin' that'll tell me who yuh are!"

"I'm just a peace-lovin' citizen," assured the prisoner earnestly. "What makes you think I'm anything but a poor, honest cowpuncher. My—you're a suspicious gent, Mister Stenger!"

"Yeah?" Stenger's voice was ominous. He stared with interest at a crumpled handbill his exploring fingers had extracted from inside the man's shirt. He turned to the silently watching riders. "Boys—listen to this—" The cowman's voice indicated vast amusement. "It's a reward notice—put out by the sheriff of Cochise—statin' that he'll pay one thousand dollars for the capture dead or alive of an hombre by name of Cal Banning whom he claims is one onery cattle-rustlin', murderin' varmint! Here's his pitcher, fellers. Any of you ever seen this bad man runnin' loose?" Stenger held the handbill against his broad chest.

Of the eight pairs of eyes that focussed on the picture of the "wanted" outlaw, only "Smoky" Kile's gleamed recognition. His jaw dropped.

"Hell, Boss. . . . It's him!" he yelled, pointing at the prisoner.

"Sure it's him," agreed Stenger, grinning. He jerked the bandanna away. "Cal Banning—in person, fellers!"

For a moment the bound man blinked at the circle of curious-eyed faces.

"Ain't disputin' this piece of paper, huh?" Stenger shook the reward notice at him.

"No denying it," admitted the young man coolly. He smiled at the riders clustered behind the cowman.

"On the run from the law, huh?" Stenger's voice was thoughtful.

"My tough luck," grumbled Banning. "Would have been clear in the Spanish Sinks—but for your outfit blockin' the pass." His gray-eyed gaze drifted to the trail-herd spreading in restless eddies over the sloping benches, and for a moment he studied the flank of a nearby bull. The brand burned into its hide was in the nature of a rude cross formed by two daggers. His gaze went back to Stenger, who was eyeing him intently.

"Cross Knife stuff, huh, Stenger? Good-lookin' bunch of beef. Must have all of four thousand and more dogies in that bunch."

The riders exchanged sly glances. Smoky Kile sneered audibly.

"Aimin' to rustle 'em from us?" he queried insolently. "Right smart hand at readin' brands, ain't yuh?"

"Have some education that way," admitted Banning mildly. "And if you want to know—the marks on your broncs has me wonderin' how come a bunch of Double S riders is nursin' Cross Knife cows through Lobo Pass. There's a question for you—Mister Smoky Kile!"

There was an ominous silence. Eight pairs of eyes regarded him with sinister interest. The red-headed Stenger was staring abstractedly at the restless herd, the growing irritation of his riders apparently unnoticed. Again it was Smoky Kile who spoke.

"Wonderin' about things sometimes ain't healthy," he remarked thinly.

"Shut up, Smoky." Stenger frowned at the swart speaker. "I'm tendin' to this bus'ness." He bent a friendly smile on Banning. "Reckon you ain't wantin' to meet up with this man-huntin' sheriff?"

"Think I'm plumb loco?" grumbled the fugitive.

Stenger chuckled. "Smoky," he said, "yuh can take yore rope off him."

Kile sulkily jerked his rawhide from the prisoner. Banning stretched stiffened muscles—grinned at the cattleman.

"Meanin' you're turnin' down a chance to collect that thousand?"

"Yuh got it figgered right," Stenger told him affably. "Fact is—can use a smart jasper like you in my outfit."

"Mister," drawled the man, "you give me new hope. I can feel that hangman's knot slippin' fast—"

"The Double S spread takes in heap big territory back in the Sinks," continued Stenger. "If my pardner says it's jake with him—yuh've done hired to a good outfit, feller."

17

"Your Double S outfit runnin' the Cross Knife, too?" Banning glanced significantly at the clamoring steers.

Again Stenger's men stiffened, narrowed eyes hostile.

"Banning!" Stenger's voice was threatening. "We understand each other—or we don't. I can use yuh if yuh want to throw in with us. If yuh don't—" The red-headed man's piggish eyes menaced the other man. "Why—we ain't waitin' to turn yuh over to the sheriff of Cochise. Get me, Banning?" His big hand closed over the butt of his six-shooter.

"Stenger," declared the young man earnestly, "I savvy you like I savvy the alphabet from A to Z— and you've hired a top-hand—name of Cal Banning."

The cattleman nodded grimly. "That's talkin' right to the point, feller. There's just one mighty healthy fact to keep in yore mind. Yuh'll see things that'll make yuh think—but so long as yuh don't think out loud—there'll be no trouble ridin' yore trail."

"Boss," chuckled the new top-hand, "I know when I'm in luck. Was sure looking for a good place to light!" He grinned cheerfully at the clustered riders. They returned his smile; all but Smoky Kile, whose somber black gaze was anything but friendly.

If Stenger noticed his foreman's disapproval of

18

the outfit's new hand, he chose to disregard it.

"Get movin', boys," ordered. He drew the glowering Smoky aside for a whispered conference and Banning turned eagerly to the bay stallion, throwing the other men a cheerful grin as they rode back to the herd. His gaze covertly sought Stenger and Kile. The latter was protesting angrily with rising voice.

"Me an' the boys has somethin' to say about things, Al!"

"There's no call for yuh to sweat, Smoky," came Stenger's placating voice. "I've figgered him out—an' if I'm wrong—it'll be just too bad for this Banning jasper." He glanced back, met the new man's narrowed stare. "Fork yuh bronc, Cal. . . . Me an' you is back-trailin' to San Carlos," he called genially.

Banning swung into the saddle and turned the stallion toward them. "All set, boss." His gaze went to Kile. "Reckon you're forgettin' somethin', mister." He held out his hand. "Don't feel like I'm dressed decent—with my guns not where I 'most always carry 'em."

There was an ugly gleam in Kile's eyes as he ungraciously handed over the two black-handled six-shooters.

"Watch yore step, cowboy," he sneered. "Yuh won't get 'em back so easy—next time."

"Listen, Kile—there ain't going to be no next time," retorted Banning, snuggling the weapons

19

into their holsters. The smile left his lips, eyes hardening to chilled steel. "And listen again, mister—you watch your own step—and tie up some of that slack lip—" The two black-handled guns seemed to leap into his hands as Kile's hand darted down to his own weapon.

"No next time," repeated Banning softly.

Kile gave him a shocked look.

"You fellers quit actin' like fool kids," growled Stenger, mingled astonishment and respect in the look he bent on his new cowhand. "Shake—an' call it a day."

"Suits me," said Banning. He slid guns back and held out his hand.

"Jake with me, cowboy." Kile's grin was forced, his hand limp. "Well, so long, boss. I'll be shovin' off."

Signaling two of the riders to join him, the Double S foreman jogged through the gap, followed by the summoned men. In another minute the bawling herd was in motion, pouring into the funnel-like ravine to the shrill, urging cries of the men riding the drag.

Chapter II

Once again Banning was riding north into the gorge, beyond which lay the vast reach of lowland known as the Spanish Sinks.

"Smoky drivin' 'em far, Stenger?" he queried casually, glancing at his big companion.

"Not so fur," returned the cattleman. "Smoky should make it come sundown—or thereabouts."

Banning nodded, his expression inscrutable. Not far from the heat-blistered sands of the Arroyo Grande lay the border. He knew that "sundown" meant somewhere in Old Mexico.

"Some slick draw yuh got, Cal," observed Stenger presently, as they clattered at a swinging trot through the winding defile. He threw a sideways glance at the stallion's rider. "Smoky's the fastest man I got—but yuh sure have him faded."

"Reckon there's not much difference," disclaimed the young man.

"Seemed kind of familiar—the way yuh pulled yore gun," mused Stenger. "Seems like I've seen that flowin' swoop of hands somewheres. Slips my mem'ry who it was. Couldn't have been you I seen doin' the trick. Never laid eyes on yuh 'til today!"

"Fellers learns the same tricks," Banning told him with a shrug.

"Reckon that's the answer." Stenger smiled grimly. "Ain't likin' yuh none the worse that yuh're a fast gun-slingin' gent."

For another hour they rode swiftly, holding little talk. Finally the gorge spewed them out on the chaparral slopes of the upper Sinks. Muttering a startled exclamation, Banning reined the stallion.

Lying near the broad swathe of hoof-torn trail was a big white steer with huge sweeping horns, and staring at the dead animal was a girl on a trim chestnut mare which shrilly returned the stallion's soft nicker. The girl's head turned in a startled look, recognition leaping to her eyes as she saw Stenger. She beckoned, calling his name.

"It's old Whitey!" she said distressfully, as they rode up. "What do you make of it, Mr. Stenger?"

She was a slim little person of that sheer and flawless beauty so often found where Erin and Old Spain have met and mingled. Banning stared, frankly absorbing her loveliness, the shining blue-black hair under the wide-brimmed felt hat, the delicious triangle of face from which sparkled great golden-brown eyes. He noted with masculine approval the grace of the exquisitely-rounded body clad in riding clothes of white linen. Under the low collar was a loosely knotted flame-colored scarf. She wore shiny black boots, inset with little silver spurs. Despite her visible distress, there was pride of race in her bearing, a haughty self-sureness in the tilt of her lovely chin.

"What do you make of it?" she repeated.

Stenger swung from his saddle and eyed the dead steer. "Sure is queer," he puzzled, shaking his head.

"Been shot," observed Banning. "Reckon that was the shootin' I heard a while back—"

Stenger's eyes flickered an angry warning. "Reckon not, Cal. . . . This critter's been dead all of three hours. Me an' you was miles away."

Banning nodded and held his peace. It was apparent that Stenger desired his silence. He had not been miles away when he heard that rifle shot shortly before his encounter with Smoky Kile.

"Sure is queer," repeated the cattleman, "providin' you're right claimin' this mossyhorn is old Whitey. Looks like him for a fact," he added. "Here, Cal—help me turn the carcass over so as we can see how the brand reads."

Banning climbed down and between them they rolled the steer over, revealing the burned outlines of the crossed daggers on the dusty white flank.

"The ol' Cross Knife, sure as yuh're born," ejaculated Stenger. His gaze studied the trampled trail. "Looks like a big bunch of dogies been shoved through here recent. Maybe your outfit's been workin' cattle down this way, Miss Anita."

The girl shook her head. "No, Mr. Stenger. The boys started roundup at Toro Lake last week— branding and cutting out a beef shipment." She looked at the dead steer, the bewilderment deepening in her eyes. "I can't puzzle it out—why old Whitey should be lying out here in the brasada. He always ranged near Toro Lake."

"How come yuh happened up here?" queried Stenger, eyeing her intently.

"I spent the week-end with Nell Brodie—over at the Box B," she explained. "We had a picnic lunch down on the Little Anita and I was taking a short cut from there back home when I saw buzzards gathering around something. I rode over—and here was poor old Whitey." She shook her head sorrowfully. "Don Mike will feel terrible. You know how he prized old Whitey—the last of the Cross Knife longhorns—and nearly twenty years old. He was a sort of link to the old days."

The three of them silently stared at the remains of the giant steer. Banning's thoughts leaped down the years to those epic times when countless thousands of similar longhorns roamed the great southwest and filled the historic Chisholm Trail with the clamor of their passing. Woven into that roaring saga of cattle and cowboy was the story of the Cross Knife—and "Don Mike" Callahan, the gallant young Irishman who had wooed and won the lovely Anita, only child of Don José Pinzon, whose famous Cross Knife brand was devised from his own proud coat of arms.

The treaty of Guadalupe Hidalgo, closing the Mexican War, had left the old don on the

American side of the new border, with less than a tenth of the vast domain granted the Pinzons by a king of Spain. His death, soon after, left the young Irish husband of Anita master of the Cross Knife, which still counted several hundred thousand acres lying between the Frio River and the Rio Grande in what became known as the Spanish Sinks.

The memory of these things swiftly came to Banning, and he eyed the girl with deepest interest, sensing that in her was the ancient blood of the Pinzons, mingled with the fiery strain of that same hard-riding, fighting son of Erin whose name had become almost legend in the Spanish Sinks as "Don Mike" of the Cross Knife Rancho.

Stenger spoke. "So yuh saw the buzzards, huh?" He gave her a sly glance and stared again at the trail winding into the gorge. "Queer about that bunch of cattle that's been through here. Cal an' me just come through the Lobo. . . . We didn't see nothin' of 'em." He nodded at the younger man. "Cal's my new top-hand—"

The girl gave Banning a friendly smile, her first direct look at him. "I'm Anita Callahan," she said, as Stenger hesitated. "You must be a good hand with cows, Mr. Banning—to be taken on as a top-hand with the Double S outfit." There was cool appraisal in the golden-brown eyes.

Banning shrugged, his own gray eyes giving

her look for look. "Sure is tough—about the old longhorn."

Her eyes clouded. "And so—so mysterious," she rejoined. "Nothing I can do—except go home and tell Don Mike—" She broke off as a shadow swept the ground at their feet, glancing quickly up at a great buzzard soaring above them, so near that they could distinctly see the repulsive naked head.

Something came floating down through the air—settled gently between the great spreading horns of the dead steer—a tail feather dropped by the carrion bird.

The girl stifled a little cry. Banning looked at her quickly. Her face was chalk white—her eyes dark with a strange dread.

"Look!" she said in a shaky voice. She pointed at the steer. "The feather—the *black feather!*"

With a little choking cry of horror, she swung the chestnut mare away and fled down the long slope over which the shadows of eventide were creeping.

Banning's wondering gaze followed until horse and girl had melted into the bristling chaparral. "Now what you reckon got into her," he said to Stenger, "chasin' off like she'd seen the devil!" He stared with narrowed eyes at the bit of black feather lying in the curve of the massive horns. "What did she mean—screechin' out about black feathers?"

Stenger rolled a sardonic eye. He seemed curiously unperturbed by the incident. "Thar's some fool talk about black feathers bringin' plenty bad luck," he answered. "Reckon it's plumb loony talk, myself," he added, contempt in his voice. He turned to his horse. "Fork yuh saddle, Cal. We gotta be movin'. Promised my pardner I'd see him in San Carlos—come sundown." The cattleman swung up to his saddle and looked round at the younger man. "Hell! Watcha doin'?" There was curious fear in the suddenly snarling voice. "Leave it lay—yuh damned fool!"

Banning straightened up from the steer, the black feather in his hand. "What's the matter, Stenger?" he asked mildly. "Thought you said something about this bein' nothin' but loony talk." He tauntingly thrust the feather into Stenger's surprised hand.

The big man's sun-reddened face turned a pasty gray. Muttering a startled oath, he flung the feather from him. "Damn yuh—pull a stunt like that agin, Banning—an' I'll sure fill yuh with plenty lead!" His hand went shakily to gun, eyes glared murderously.

Banning's astonished expression seemed to calm him; he forced a grin. "Yuh know how it is, Cal," he said sheepishly. "No hombre likes a bad luck jinx handed him—even for a fool joke—not that I take stock in 'em, at that."

"I'm bettin' the same way," laughed the cowboy.

"Here's provin' no black feather casts shadows of fear 'cross my trail." He retrieved the reputed token of ill-luck and stuck it inside the band of his Stetson.

"Listen close," growled the cattleman. "Black feathers ain't popular in the Spanish Sinks. Yuh ain't wearin' that jinx if yuh aims to ride with me."

"You're the boss, Stenger," chuckled Banning. "Just the same, I've a hunch I've found me a good-luck piece and I sure ain't throwing my luck away." He pulled the feather from his hat and tucked it inside his flannel shirt.

They rode at a steady trot down the trail that twisted through the mesquite. The sun had settled below the mountain ridge behind them; soft twilight mantled the stark chaparral reaching down to the flats. Lights twinkled in the distance. Stenger eased his bulk in the saddle.

"San Carlos," he told his companion. "Can yuh beat it?" he added gleefully. "That gal runnin' acrost that damned ol' mossyhorn the way she did?"

"Who is she?" Banning's voice was casual, uninterested.

"The gal?" Stenger gave his questioner a sharp glance. "She's Don Mike's granddaughter."

"Sure is one good-luckin' female," declared the cowboy enthusiastically.

Stenger grunted. "Listen," he said, "I'm warnin'

yuh—keep off. There's a better man than you—dallyin' his rope for Anita Callahan."

"I'm right smart with a rope my own self," retorted the young man coolly. He gave his employer a cautious glance. "Why did you tell her that we didn't see any cattle in the pass?"

"Wasn't aimin' for her to know," said Stenger frankly. He grinned. "Had me sweatin'—her findin' that ol' longhorn. Should have left the ol' dogie back at Toro Lake."

"So you did shoot him?" Banning spoke softly.

"Sure did," grunted the cattleman. "Was too old to travel—slowed up the herd."

"I get you." Banning nodded. "Meanin' you pulled off a job of rustlin', huh, Stenger?"

"Meanin' no such damn-fool thing," snorted the Double S man. His little red eyes shot his new top-hand a furtive, sideways glance. "Don Mike an' me made a deal that the gal ain't s'posed to know about."

"How come—you don't want her to know?"

"Don Mike's got 'em mortgaged to old Ace Coons. Was scared Ace would seize 'em for debt, an' framed with me to make out they was rustled." Stenger grinned. "Don Mike's an old jasper—an' a friend. I'd go the limit to help him—an' remember, Cal—I'm spillin' somethin' that you ain't repeatin'—savvy?"

"Framed to rustle his own cattle, huh?" Banning

whistled amazement. "That's sure getting out from under, Stenger. But what will this Ace Coons bird think of the raw deal you're pullin'? Won't he suspect?"

"That's the joke, feller!" The big cattleman chuckled. "Old Ace'll just natcherly blame the King Buzzard gang that's been rustlin' the Spanish Sinks to the bone. Reckon that's what the gal thought when she lamped that blamed black feather layin' there on ol' Whitey. That's what scared her. She got the notion right off that maybe the King Buzzard had been raidin' the Cross Knife while she was visitin over at the Box B. Couldn't have worked out better!"

Banning's voice was puzzled. "What do you mean, Stenger? What's a black feather got to do with this rustlin' King Buzzard gang?"

"It's the King Buzzard's callin' card," explained Stenger. "If yuh find one layin' on yore door-step—don't waste no time arguin' about it, feller. Fork yore bronc an' high-tail it pronto."

"Meanin' what?"

"Meanin' that to disobey the warnin' of the black feather is sure one good way to commit suicide," Stenger assured him. "There's some that's tried to buck the King Buzzard—an' now they ain't here—nor nowhere else."

Banning nodded, patted one of his black-handled guns. "Reckon that's why you took a chance—hiring me, huh, Stenger? Figgered you could use a good gun-slinger—these days—and nights."

"We're needin' good gun-slingers in the Sinks," admitted the cattleman dryly. "The King Buzzard ain't troubled me none—yet—but yuh never can tell what he'll pull off." He grinned. "Now yuh savvy the real reason why I got yuh to pull that dang feather from yore hat. Don't want folks sayin' my new top-hand is one of the King Buzzard gang." He gave the cowboy a sinister smile. "Shake up yore bronc, feller. Them lights yonder says there's good likker waitin' for us in San Carlos."

Chapter III

It was dark when they rode into the dusty street that was the border town of San Carlos. The night was clear—without a moon—the deep blue arch of sky ablaze with coldly glittering stars.

The drab little street was strangely quiet, the shoddy frame buildings somber walls of darkness, with here and there the warm glow of lamplight behind curtained windows. The silence struck Banning as unnatural—ominous—the deadly calm preceding a storm's devastating violence. He looked uneasily at his companion. Stenger was staring furtively at a lighted window of one of the larger, more pretentious buildings. Banning's quick glance read the black lettering on the glass:

ASA COONS
LOANS
CATTLE—LAND

His glance prolonged to an interested stare. Thrown in silhouette on the drawn shade was the figure of a girl. It seemed to Banning that her attitude was that of one in dire despair—that she was weeping.

Stenger's voice drew his attention.

"Here's where we light an' likker, Cal."

He reined his horse in front of a building across the street, almost opposite the office of Asa Coons. It was a garish front, with a kerosene street lamp throwing a pale glow on the swing doors. Hung above the entrance was a sign—a crude picture of a horse's head, with flying mane and blowing nostrils.

Some half score cow ponies were tied in front of the place. Banning was suddenly struck with the fact that numerous other horses were clustered at the various hitching racks scattered along the street, indicating that many riders were in town. A fact deepening the mystery of the all-pervading quiet.

"My pardner's place," Stenger informed him, nodding at the gaudy front of the Horsehead Bar. He swung down stiffly. "Sassoon'll want to look yuh over, Cal." He stretched his huge frame, darting another furtive glance at the lighted window across the street, and muttering profane desire for immediate liquid refreshment.

Tying their horses, they turned to the swing doors from which welled a subdued murmur of men's voices. Stenger halted his stride and stared attentively at an old Indian squatting on the board sidewalk.

"Whatcha want, Chico?"

The Indian gestured across the street. "Sassoon—him tellum me him want see you. He tellum you come heap quick."

33

"Sassoon!" Stenger's voice was worried. "Yuh mean he's over at Ace Coons' place, Chico?"

The Indian nodded. Muttering an oath, Stenger swung on his heel and started across the street, gesturing for Banning to follow.

The jingle and rasp of their spurs warned listening ears. The office door jerked open, revealing the tall, lithe figure of a man framed against yellow lamplight.

"Hello, Al." He addressed Stenger in low tones. "Thought that would be you. Told Chico to watch out for you." He drew aside, giving Banning a sleepy-eyed glance.

The latter scarcely noticed him. His gaze had leaped to the girl, leaning wearily back in a big office chair, her eyes closed, long jet lashes in startling contrast to the ivory pallor of her face. The Cross Knife girl—Anita Callahan!

Beyond her, at a paper-littered desk, was an elderly man who stared searchingly at Stenger's companion from behind amber-tinted spectacles perched on a beak-like nose. He sat in a peculiar, huddled posture, long, flat, hairless head sunk forward on gaunt, wide shoulders from which loosely hung a shiny black alpaca coat. His yellow stare went to the girl.

"Is this the man, Miss Callahan?" His voice was surprisingly sonorous, bell-toned.

The girl looked briefly at Banning.

"Yes, Mr. Coons."

34

Stenger stirred uneasily—looked at Sassoon. "Banning's a new hand I took on, Joe," he told the latter. He eyed round at the cowboy. "Cal—meet Joe Sassoon—my pardner in the Double S."

Sassoon smiled, showing even white teeth under a dark smudge of mustache. He was in striking contrast to the roughly-dressed, brutal-faced Stenger; fastidiously, almost foppishly clothed. The raven hair, sleepy, dark, liquid eyes, and the warmth of his coloring, spoke of Spanish blood. There was catlike grace in the lithe body—a feline stealth in the heavy-lidded eyes.

"I leave the hiring to you, Al," he said. He looked down at the crumpled little figure in the chair. "Something terrible has happened, Al—" His voice lost its softness. "Ace wants to ask you some questions—" Sassoon paused, looked at the bald-headed man behind the desk. "You tell them, Ace."

"Don Mike has been murdered," said the money-lender. The deep-toned voice was like the dirging of a funeral bell—seemed to wreck the girl's fortitude. She uttered a stifled little cry.

Sassoon bent down to her quickly. "Don't let it get you, Anita."

"It's all too—too horrible," she told him brokenly. "I—I can't endure it!"

"Now, my dear," broke in the big, kindly voice of Asa Coons; "you must bear up—or you'll be sick—unable to help us bring these cowardly killers to justice—"

She straightened up—stared at him tensely. "Yes—of course—I mustn't break—now. These men must be punished." Her dark eyes blazed. "They must be hunted down—hanged!"

Coons nodded. "We are all with you, my dear. We will never rest—until justice has been done." His bespectacled gaze slowly swept their faces and fastened on Banning, the lamplight reflecting on the amber lenses, making them shine like huge, yellow, staring eyes.

"Stranger here, aren't you, Banning?"

"You might call me that," admitted the cowboy, uneasy under that yellow-eyed look.

"How did you happen to employ him, Stenger?" Coons shifted his gaze to the cattleman. "We have to be careful about strangers—way things are these days."

"Met Cal back in Lobo Pass," explained Stenger. "Said he was lookin' for a job." The cattleman scowled. "Don't figger out yore talk, Ace. Cal don't know nothin' about this Don Mike killin'."

"I asked Joe to have you in, Stenger, because Miss Callahan tells me that she met you—and this young stranger—on her way home from the Box B. She'd just found that old longhorn of Don Mike's—lying out there in the brush—shot through the head."

Stenger nodded. "Sure was queer—that old mossyhorn lyin' there—"

"Not so queer, Stenger. In fact, rather obvious. Miss Callahan noticed something else—something sinister—lying there—"

"A buzzard's tail-feather," interrupted the cattleman impatiently. "Sure—the buzzard dropped it—flyin' round over our heads while we was standin' there." He laughed, rolled his eyes at Banning.

"This is no time to laugh," reproved the banker. "We know the feather was a coincidence, but it made Miss Callahan apprehensive. She knew that her grandfather had received a warning—a warning which he had chosen to ignore. The mystery of the steer—the signs of cattle recently pushed through the Lobo—apparently failed to rouse Miss Callahan's fears. It was the coincidence of the black feather that gave her the first inkling of disaster at the Cross Knife." Coons shook his head sadly. "She found Don Mike lying dead on his own doorstep—riddled with bullets. A raid, Stenger. . . . Three of his riders—dead in the corrals . . . the cook and an Indian boy in the kitchen—knifed . . . all dead."

"The—the hell—you say!" stammered the cattleman. His face was ashen. "Reckon it was the—the King Buzzard gang—Ace?"

"Stuck inside the shirt of each of them was a black feather," Coons told him solemnly.

"The King Buzzard's callin' card for sartain," muttered Stenger, rolling his eyes at Banning.

"Miss Callahan did the only thing possible—came to town as fast as her horse could move—to me. I've sent Doc Spicer out to the ranch to take care of the—of things there. Jim Brodie was in town—and some of his boys—when Anita brought the news. She told us that most of the Cross Knife outfit was at Toro Lake—working cattle. Jim and his men rode out there—" Coons shook his bald head pessimistically. "Afraid they'll be too late. The King Buzzard works fast. . . . By this time the gang has made a clean sweep of the Cross Knife."

"Anita told us there were signs of a drive through the pass. That right, Al?"

It was Sassoon's soft voice speaking, eyes questioning his partner.

"Why—yes—" replied Stenger. "There was plenty sign—but we didn't see no cattle when we come through the Lobo." He looked at Banning. "Ain't that right, feller?"

"Sure was plenty sign," admitted the cowboy sullenly.

Sassoon nodded. "That means the gang's crossed the border by now—and the Cross Knife cattle with 'em."

"No doubt about that," boomed the money-lender. He looked at Stenger. "Nothing more you can tell us, Al?"

"Nary a thing," growled the Double S man. "Reckon Cal an' me might as well be movin' over to the Horsehead. We ain't et yet." He looked at the girl. "Sure sorry about—about Don Mike—an' all, Miss Anita," he added awkwardly. "If there's anything I can do—yuh can sure count on me—an' that goes for every man on the Double S payroll. Ain't that right, Joe?"

"I've already given Anita that assurance," Sassoon told him.

The girl thanked them with a tired, grave little smile, her glance lingering for an instant on Banning.

"Come on, Cal," grunted Stenger. "Let's go." He turned to the door.

"One moment, Al." The banker's yellow glare halted the cattleman.

"Huh?" Stenger scowled. "What's on yore mind, Ace?"

"Your men," said Coons severely. "They can't do this town any good—with their carousing and gunplay. I've too many interests here to have your drunken riders shooting up the place every payday."

"They don't mean no harm, Ace," protested Stenger. "Yuh can't blame the boys for feelin' good paydays. They work hard—an' play hard."

"It's that foreman of yours—Smoky Kile," grumbled Coons. "Next time he pulls off gunplay like he did the other night in the Horsehead— he'll answer to me."

"The feller had it comin'," declared Stenger. "He'd no bus'ness insinooatin' Smoky was in with the King Buzzard gang."

"I didn't know that, Al. . . . Well—perhaps Smoky was justified in killing the man."

"I'll say he was!" retorted the cattleman. "This feller, Simkins, was one of them squatters down on Frio Creek that was burned out by the King Buzzard gang. He jumped Smoky—claimed he'd seen Smoky with the gang that night, an' went for his gun—"

"All right, Al," interrupted Coons. "Let the matter drop. I'd do what Smoky did—if any man said things like that to me. Nevertheless," added the banker sternly, "even if there is no sheriff in San Carlos—we must have law and order—and that goes for you, too, Sassoon."

"You run your old cattle loan business, Ace— and leave me to mind my business as I see fit," sneered the gambler. He looked apologetically at the girl. "We're forgetting Miss Callahan. . . . She needs rest."

Coons nodded. "Right, Joe. . . . Perhaps you will see her to the hotel. Hank's woman will make her comfortable."

"I'm not going to the hotel," demurred Anita as Sassoon stepped toward her. "My place is at the ranch—with—with poor Don Mike."

"My dear Anita—you can't stay out there all alone," expostulated Sassoon.

"I'll wait for Jim Brodie," she told him firmly. "He'll be back from Toro Lake before long. He'll stay with me—and we can get Nell over." She sprang from the chair and went to the window, pressing close to Banning. "I couldn't possibly think of going *anywhere*—until I hear from Jim Brodie. I want to know what has happened to Clem Sanders—and the boys!" She stared dejectedly into the darkness.

"Something comin' up the street," muttered the cowboy.

The white triangle of her face came slowly from the window, golden brown eyes reaching over her shoulder to his. He nodded answer to the eager question in the look.

"Horses," he told her. "It's horses you're hearin'—and coming fast."

They stood, staring at each other, ears keyed to delicate pitch. Behind them, Sassoon and Stenger exchanged startled glances, then looked at Asa Coons. The bald-headed banker was apparently lost in thought, chin sunk on breast, fingers beating a soft tattoo against the desk.

The faint whisper of sound soughing through the night swelled quickly to the unmistakable drumming of horses' hoofs. Sassoon flashed a glittering look at Stenger. Both men moved quickly toward the door. The girl was there first.

She jerked it open. Smothering an oath, Stenger ducked from the path of light. Sassoon sank back into the shadows, his hand slipping inside his coat, eyes narrowed to cat-like slits. Observing that Stenger's hand had gone to his holstered gun, Banning slid fingers over the handles of his own six-shooters and surged to the girl framed in the open doorway.

"Wouldn't stand there in the light," he warned. "Might be the Buzzard gang—"

She shook her head, peering intently up the street. "It's Jim Brodie," she told them; and then excitedly: "Clem Sanders is with them!"

Her hand unconsciously clutched his arm, drawing him close to her side, and together they stood in the blaze of lamplight, watching the approaching riders.

Apparently doubtful of the girl's recognition of Brodie and his men, Sassoon and Stenger made no move toward the open door. There was an expression of something like terror in the cattleman's little red eyes. He licked his lips—darted a sideways glance at Coons. The money-lender had not stirred from his seat behind the desk. There was something formidable in the untouchable serenity of the man as he sat there motionless as a Buddha, amber spectacles gleaming like twin yellow eyes.

Chapter IV

Across the street, men poured from the Horsehead Bar, thronging the sidewalk, watching wordlessly as the group of riders halted in front of the open office door. Their silence struck Banning as uncanny—as though every man there was in the thrall of a ghastly fear.

A tall, gaunt man with a drooping grizzled mustache headed the riders and was the first to swing from the saddle. Observing the girl anxiously peering from the doorway, he waved a reassuring hand.

"Be with you in a minute," he called. "Got Clem with us. . . . He wants to see you."

Two of the men were easing one of the riders from his saddle.

"Oh, he's hurt! Clem's hurt!" exclaimed Anita. Her little hand tightened convulsively on Banning's arm. She looked up at him, panic in the lovely eyes. "And Doc Spicer—out at the ranch—"

"Don't you worry," he comforted. "I'm right good at doctorin' gun wounds myself." He brushed past her and joined the little group in the street.

The wounded Clem Sanders was a stocky young person, with crisp fair hair and clear blue

43

eyes in a frank, open face at this moment deathly pale as he leaned against the saddle.

"Leave me be," he good-naturedly remonstrated with his helpers. "No sense makin' her think I'm hurt bad."

They stood aside, eyeing him worriedly as he turned from the horse, gritting teeth against the pain that left him weak and dizzy. Banning reached him with a quick stride.

"Here, feller—lean against that," he said curtly. He braced an arm under Sanders' shoulders and gently propelled him up to the sidewalk. Anita darted out.

"Let me help!"

She slipped an arm round the wounded man's lean waist and slowly they got him into the office.

"You boys wait for me over at the Horsehead," the tall, gaunt man told the riders. "An' watch your step . . . no drinkin'." He hurried to join the wounded Cross Knife foreman in the office. Grimly silent, the Box B men turned across the street, to the swing doors through which the crowd was sullenly thronging.

"Rest him on the couch," Coons said in his big kindly voice. He pointed to an old horsehair sofa. They eased him down gently. Sanders grinned apologetically at the girl's concerned face.

"Plumb foolish—me actin' like a sick colt. Ain't hurt none at all to worry about."

"Hush," she told him. "Of course you're hurt." She looked distressfully at the blood-soaked shirt.

"I'm takin' a look at that," said Banning. Ignoring Sanders' protests, he ripped the shirt open, pulling it down from the shoulder.

"Easy there, cowboy," muttered the Cross Knife man faintly. "Yuh ain't skinnin' a calf."

The tall, gaunt man had paused near the door and stood silently watching the proceedings. Stenger and Sassoon, standing on either side of the door, and slightly behind him, studied the massive, seamed face intently, as though striving to read the rancher's thoughts. Coons, from his chair behind the desk, was the first to address him.

"Where did you pick him up, Brodie? Haven't had time to make it to Toro Lake and back."

Brodie jerked around and stared at the banker. "Didn't go to Toro Lake," he answered. "Met Clem headin' for town—or tryin' to. . . . Was about to keel off his bronc when we run into him." The rancher's frowning gaze suddenly observed Sassoon and Stenger. "What's the matter with you birds? Might think I was the King Buzzard—the way you're actin'."

Sassoon shrugged—moved toward the couch. "No telling when that devil may pop out of the box, Brodie. Al Stenger was getting all set for a fight when your outfit rode in just now." He smiled sardonically. "Al acts like the King

Buzzard's got him spotted for the next black feather."

"Not if I see him first," grunted the Double S man.

Brodie snorted. "Gettin' fed up with this King Buzzard talk," he declared, following Sassoon to the sofa.

Stenger's wicked little eyes sparkled, lips lifting in something like a snarl. Leaning massive shoulders against the closed door, he stealthily watched the little group at the sofa.

"You're in luck, mister," Banning congratulated the Cross Knife foreman. "That hunk of lead went in between two ribs—and clean out—without nicking a bone. Losin' some blood is about the sum total of the damage—and you get off cheap at that. An inch lower—and you wouldn't be here to tell us the story."

"Bled like a fool hawg," admitted Sanders feebly. "Couldn't stop that bleedin'."

"Need some water—and iodine—and something clean for a bandage," said Banning, looking round at the others.

"Needs a good shot of whiskey—that's what he needs," commented Stenger from the door. "I'll go get yuh a quart, Clem. Reckon the Horsehead'll stand yuh a drink, eh, Joe?" He grinned at Sassoon, who nodded.

"Sure—go get a bottle, Al," he assented.

"Don't drink the stuff," protested the wounded

man. "Just get me tied up—that's all I ask."

"Well—I'm needin' a drink—if you ain't," grumbled Stenger. He pulled the door open. "Come on over, Banning—when yuh get through playin' doctor. I'll be at the Horsehead." The door closed behind him.

For the first time, Asa Coons left his chair, slowly crossing the room on a pair of crutches. Banning's eyes widened in a surprised stare. The San Carlos banker was a cripple—with a twisted leg dangling helplessly.

"You'll find a roll of antiseptic bandage on a shelf in the back room," he told them, "and iodine. There's fresh water in the bucket."

"I'll get it," offered Sassoon. He hurried away.

Leaning on his crutches, Coons stared down at the wounded man. "Too bad," he muttered, and then with a worried glance at Anita, "Sit down, my dear—or why don't you go over to the hotel as I suggested? You need rest—and there's nothing you can do here."

"No," demurred the girl. "I want to hear about what happened—at Toro Lake." She sank into the chair that Brodie slid toward her, thanking him with a smile. "I can go home with you, can't I, Mr. Brodie?"

"You bet you can, girl," declared the big ranchman heartily. "Nell wouldn't think of you doing anything else. You're welcome at the Box B as long as you want to stay."

Clem Sanders turned his head and looked enquiringly at them, his eyes startlingly blue in his white face.

"Why ain't you goin' home to the Cross Knife?" he queried suspiciously. "What's wrong—there? Where's Don Mike? . . . I've sure got a heap of bad news to tell him," he added miserably.

The girl drew back, eyes questioning Banning. His look warned her to silence. It was Coons who answered him.

"Your news won't hurt Don Mike, son," he said solemnly. "Don Mike is dead—killed by the raiders—"

The Cross Knife foreman sat up, eyes filling with horror. "Killed—Don Mike—!" He uttered a strangled cry—collapsed in a faint.

"What did you go and tell him for?" exclaimed Brodie furiously. "Didn't you see Banning warnin' us not to let him know?"

With a frantic glance at the banker, Anita had leaped from her chair—was bending over the unconscious man. "Oh, he's dead—he's dead!" she gasped. Her eyes implored Banning.

"Just passed out for a bit," assured the latter. "Wasn't strong enough to stand a shock like that." He gave Coons a stormy look. "Should have known better than that, mister."

Sassoon's return with bandages and iodine—and the water, interrupted further recriminations.

With an apologetic shrug, Coons hobbled back to his desk.

"There," announced Banning presently, as he finished dressing and bandaging the wound. "He's coming out of it." He smiled down at the patient. "How she feel, feller?"

"Seems like I've seen you before—somewhere," answered Sanders, a puzzled expression in his eyes.

"Reckon not," returned Banning. "Never laid eyes on you—and I never forget a face."

"I'm that way, too," muttered the Cross Knife foreman. "Never forget a face myself." He rolled his eyes, meeting the anxious gaze of the girl. "So they got—Don Mike—"

"We won't talk about it now, Clem," she begged him. "Wait until you are stronger—"

"They got Curly—and old Chuck," said Clem feebly. "I'd sent Bert—and Pete—and Buck back for a fresh string of broncs. The rest of us was holdin' the herd down in the old dry slough at Toro Lake when we was jumped. . . . Saw Curly and Chuck go down . . . and then I passed out. . . . Didn't get a chance to pull a gun. When I come to—the cows was gone—and there was poor old Curly lyin' there dead . . . and old Chuck—each of 'em with a black feather stuck in his shirt." Sanders paused, fumbled with a shaky hand at his own shirt. "Found a feather stickin' in my shirt, too. . . . Reckon they thought I was dead. I got it with me—in my pocket."

"Here she is." Banning pulled a little black feather from the pocket of the blood-soaked shirt.

There was a silence, broken by Coons' bell-toned voice.

"You're the first man to get a black feather—and live to tell about it, young man."

"I'm keepin' it," gasped young Sanders, reaching weakly for the sinister token. "Some day—I'll be returnin' it to this King Buzzard—with plenty hot lead—" He looked at Brodie. "Tell me, Jim—did they get Bert—and the others?"

The rancher's grim nod answered him.

"Damn him!" gasped the Cross Knife foreman; "Damn the King Buzzard!"

He tried to sit up. Banning gently restrained him. "Better get him to bed somewhere," he advised Brodie.

The ranchman nodded. "You lay still—and quit that fightin' talk," he admonished Sanders. "An' listen, young feller—I'm takin' you back to the Box B—" Brodie winked at Anita. "Reckon you won't kick none—havin' Nell strokin' your head an' feedin' you chicken broth an' makin' you feel like a hero, huh?"

"Listens good," admitted Sanders, a pleased expression wiping the grim lines from his face. "You can't get me over to the Box B too quick, Jim. I mean if Anita is comin' with us," he added.

"Sure she is," said Brodie. "I'll go over and get the boys. We'll dig up a buckboard for you to ride easy in . . . Anita can hold your poor head in her lap. Huh, Anita?"

"Of course," agreed the girl with a faint smile. The thought of doing something for somebody cheered her for a moment, then her eyes darkened with pain. "I don't know, though, Mr. Brodie," she faltered. "My place really is at home—with—with Don Mike."

"Doc Spicer is there, girl. You mustn't think of going back to the Cross Knife tonight," argued Brodie. He considered a moment. "Tell you what—we'll get you and Clem home first—then I'll ride over to the Cross Knife with one of the boys."

Anita hesitated. "If you think it is best," she said doubtfully.

"It's settled," the big ranchman told her firmly. He turned to the door. Banning followed him. The girl called to him gratefully.

"Thank you, Mr. Banning. I won't forget what you've done for us—for Clem Sanders."

Banning halted—looked at her. "Let me know if there's anything else I can do," he said.

"Miss Callahan has plenty of friends in this town, Banning," broke in Sassoon icily. "The Double S boys are all ready to do Miss Callahan a service, mister."

The cowboy shrugged. "I'm one of 'em,

51

Sassoon," he said coolly. "The Double S is writin' my paycheck, too." He moved on toward the door, where Brodie had paused to listen.

Sassoon hesitated, his gaze going to Coons. The bald-headed banker had again assumed his peculiar air of detachment, gaunt, wide shoulders huddled low in the big chair, chin sunk on breast, fingers tapping the desk.

Sassoon's eyes narrowed. "Say—Brodie," he called hurriedly. "I've an idea!"

Brodie glanced back, hand on door-knob.

"I suggest that Banning and myself ride out to the ranch—and see to things. No need for you to go to the Cross Knife tonight." Sassoon looked at the girl. "I'm sure Anita will feel safer—with you at the Box B."

Brodie hesitated. "It's up to her," he said gruffly. "If she wants it that way—"

Her expression indicated approval of the plan, and Sassoon hurried to join the men waiting at the door. Coons lifted his head.

"Brodie," he boomed, "where were you this morning—when the raid was pulled off?"

"What do you mean?" demanded the ranchman huffily. "What's the idea—questionin' me?"

"A natural question, Brodie. There's a lot of mystery about this King Buzzard. Nobody knows his identity. . . . Every man in the Spanish Sinks is probably wondering if he is neighbor to the monster responsible for this reign of terror."

Brodie's face was purple. "What's that, Coons?" he shouted. "Insinuating that maybe I'm the King Buzzard?" He took an angry step toward the desk.

"Now, Brodie," protested Coons mildly. "I merely asked you a natural question—a question that men will be asking other men—about their movements this morning."

"Maybe you're right, Coons," admitted Brodie, cooling. "Matter of fact—I was down on Frio Creek with some of the boys—roundin' up strays." He yanked the door open and strode out, glowering, followed by Banning and Sassoon.

"The danged suspicious old Four-Eyes," he fumed as they went across the street. "Sittin' there and suspicioning folks thataway."

"What does he wear those colored glasses for?" Banning wanted to know.

"Got weak eyes, he says," explained Sassoon.

"Nobody's ever seen him without 'em," added Brodie.

"Wonder what his eyes look like?" murmured the cowboy. "Sure seems a queer duck. Can't make him out."

"Asa Coons is the richest man in the Spanish Sinks," Sassoon told him.

"And what that old Shylock ain't got a mortgage on—ain't worth the price of a dead maverick," snorted Brodie.

"Meaning you're one of his clients, Brodie?" sneered the gambler.

The big Box B man bristled. "Anyone says I owe Ace Coons a dollar is a liar," he rasped. "I've seen too many of 'em cringing at his door, Sassoon."

"Maybe you're wise," laughed Sassoon. "You've got the makings of a real ranch in the Box B."

"Don't I know?" agreed Brodie. "And don't old Coons know it? He's tried to buy me out more than once—at somethin' like a dime on the dollar. . . . The old skinflint "

There was an unmistakable note of fear in the ranchman's voice that made Banning look at him curiously.

CHAPTER V

"Thar's blood on the moon," direfully proclaimed a weazened old cowman to the crowd sullenly glooming in the long barroom of the Horsehead. "Vultures' wings is castin' shadders acrost the land," he told them.

An ominous hush greeted the ancient rider's shrill utterance. Men's eyes went blank, furtively masking thoughts that might betray dangerous suspicions. To voice such suspicions could swiftly bring the fateful black feather to one's own doorstep.

"Old age is givin' yuh a loose tongue, Windy," frowned the barman, nervously mopping his mahogany with a damp rag. He darted an uneasy glance at a group of cowboys clustered round a card table near the door—Box B men, waiting Jim Brodie's expected summons.

Mindful of his orders to refrain from drinking, they sat in sullen silence, regarding the inebriated little man at the bar with hostile eyes.

"How come yuh drinkin' solo, Windy?" queried the bartender softly. "Been fired from the Box B—or somethin'—that the boys is givin' yuh the cold shoulder?"

Windy Ben Allen teetered drunkenly on the high heels of his worn boots. "Ain't been fired," he retorted shrilly. "I up an' quit the Box B, Monty."

"Yuh don't say!" exclaimed the bartender, suddenly attentive.

"Yes suh—quit Jim Brodie cold," affirmed the old man. "An' after me ridin' for him more'n twenty years." He turned to glare at his late associates, elbow upsetting the whiskey glass just replenished by the barman.

"Now see what yuh done," grumbled the latter, wet cloth slapping the puddle of liquor. "What yuh go an' quit Brodie for, Windy?"

"He aimed to make a pump-tender out of me," complained Ben. "Cause I ain't as young as some—an' ain't much good for ridin' since I got busted in that thar stampede, Jim aimed to keep me like a exile at the ol' Sand Hill camp, pumpin' water for a lot of danged cows. That's gratitood for yuh, Monty—treatin' me thataways after all these years. Why, Monty—I helped Jim Brodie mark the first longhorn to wear the Box B on its hide!"

"Sure ain't human," sympathized the bartender in a low voice. He refilled the glass.

"Rode stirrup to stirrup with Jim when the Box B was a infant," reminisced Windy Ben almost tearfully. "Them was he-man days, Monty—what with rustlers an' stampedes an' brandburners—an' everythin'."

"Not so loud, old timer," warned the man behind the bar. "Here comes Brodie . . . he's liable to take yuh apart if he hears yuh bawlin' him out."

Followed by Sassoon and Banning, the Box B owner pushed in through the swing doors. The sight of Windy Ben hugging the bar seemed to enrage him. He halted—glared contemptuously at his late employee.

"Joe," he said loudly to Sassoon, "what's the idea—allowin' a double-crossin' little skunk to contaminate a decent place like the Horsehead?"

Again Windy Ben's whiskey splashed across the bar, thin glass tinkling to pieces on the floor as he reached for his gun.

"Go for yore smoke-pot, mister!" he yelled. "I'll dang well larn yuh thar's a few teeth left in this old wolf's haid!"

With a panther-like movement, Sassoon interposed his dapper person between the two men.

"Put up that gun, Windy," he ordered quietly. "No gunplay in my place—or you'll answer to me." He turned cold eyes on the glowering ranchman. "No need to insult the old man, Brodie. Ben Allen is always welcome in the Horsehead."

"I've quit him!" howled the old cowboy. "Me an' the Box B is through!"

"What's that?" roared Brodie. "Quit—you say? Why—you sawed-off useless coyote—I fired you—and fired you plenty!" With an angry snort, the tall ranchman turned to his silently watchful men grouped at the card table.

"Ain't that gratitood for yuh, Mister Sassoon?"

hiccoughed Windy Ben tearfully. "Usin' me thataways—after the pal I been to him!"

The saloon man eyed him thoughtfully—swiftly surveyed the long room.

"Where's Stenger?" he asked the bartender.

"Back in yore office, boss," returned Monte, industriously polishing his bar.

"Tell him I want him, Banning," directed Sassoon, indicating a rear door.

Banning went to the door, observing out of the corner of his eye that one of the Box B men was hurrying out after a brief whispered conference with Brodie. The latter sat down.

"Sent Slim over to Larsen's for a buckboard," he told Sassoon. "Soon as he gets hitched, we'll pull out for the ranch—with Clem and the girl." He shook his grizzled head. "Nasty business—this Don Mike killin'."

Sassoon nodded, continuing his silent scrutiny of old Windy Ben who was drunkenly arguing with the bartender about payment for the spilled liquor. Stenger lurched from the private room, enquiring gaze on his partner.

"Whatcha want, Joe?"

His utterance was thick. It was obvious that the Double S man had been making up for lost time since leaving the office across the street. Sassoon gave him an ugly look.

"Weren't you telling me you needed a new cook out at the ranch, Al?" he asked.

58

"Me—needin' a cook?" Stenger's voice was puzzled. "Don't get yuh, Joe."

"You told me Tubby Jones was quittin'," reminded Sassoon, significantly, it seemed to Banning.

"Oh—yeah—sure—that's right," stuttered Stenger. He grinned stupidly. "Clean forgot about ol' Tubby wantin' to lay off for a spell. Sure we need a cook."

"Ben Allen's needing a job," Sassoon said, nodding at the old man noisily bickering with Monte. He raised his voice. "Ben—listen. . . . How'd you like a job—cooking for the Double S outfit?"

Windy Ben turned his wrinkled, leathery face and stared amazedly at the speaker.

"You aimin' to inshult me, mister?" he demanded with drunken gravity. "I ain't cookin' for no bow-legged cowpokes, Sasshoon."

"Don't get me wrong, Ben," smiled Sassoon. "I've heard tales about the way you can cook. They say there isn't a man in the Sinks can throw a meal together as tasty as you can. You're just the cook we want, old timer. We feed the Double S boys high."

Windy Ben regarded him with owlish solemnity. "Thash right, Sasshoon," he hiccoughed. "I can out-ride an' out-rope an' out-cook any danged hombre in ten states." He shook his head. "But I ain't takin' no cookin' job. No suh—me—I'm gettin' me a better lay-out." Ben gave the room a maudlin grin—nodded mysteriously. "I'll go so far to tell yuh gents here gathered in joyful occasion that maybe I'll join up with this King Buzzard hombre. Reckon thar's right smart pickin's whar his feathers 'light."

Again grim silence greeted his reference to the sinister terror of the Spanish Sinks, blank faces masking suspicions their owners feared to reveal. Two men alone failed to dissemble. One was Cal Banning, gray eyes covertly studying the bibulous Windy Ben. The other man was Brodie. The latter leaped from his chair angrily.

"You onery little snake!" he rasped. "The boys tell me that's twice runnin' you go an' mention this here murderin' King Buzzard. It goes to prove you're knowin' him better'n an honest man should—"

"Brodie," broke in the cold voice of Sassoon. "You seem to overlook the fact that our friend is— is merely celebrating in his own way. . . . He doesn't mean it seriously."

"He's no friend of mine!" roared the incensed ranchman. "As for celebratin'—what's he celebratin'? Is he celebratin' his stated intentions of joinin' up with the King Buzzard gang that's just killed old Don Mike—the finest man in the Spanish Sinks?" He glared at the old cowboy. "I've listened plenty to you, Ben Allen! Your talk don't make a hit with me! My own Box B

60

outfit neighbors the Cross Knife—and that means your buzzard gang of killers has me marked for the next black feather, I reckon."

Brodie eyed fiercely round the room at the mask-like faces. "I'll be ready for 'em," he challenged. "And as for you—Ben Allen! I'm warnin' you, feller."

"An' I'm warnin' you—Jim Brodie," shrilled Windy Ben. "I'll sure be ridin' yore trail—yuh ongrateful ol' catamount!" He gazed round with a silly smile which centered for the merest instant on Banning.

The young cowboy's eyes narrowed. He could have sworn that the old puncher's leathery eyelid twitched in a sly wink. The next moment, Windy Ben lurched up to him, skinny hand reaching out. "Waal, young feller—ain't been seein' you round before. Recent in the Sinks, huh?" he greeted noisily.

"Cal Banning has just hired on with the Double S," Stenger informed him with a sly grin. "Cal is some dainty about his eats, Ben. That's why I'm kinda hopin' yuh'll change yore mind about that cookin' job, ol' timer."

"That's right, Ben," Banning chimed in gravely.

"Waal—now that yuh put it up to me thataway—maybe I'll take yuh up on the deal," ruminated Ben. He rubbed his thinning hair. "Yes," he decided, nodding his head, "yuh've done hired a cook, Stenger." He hooked an arm inside Banning's and lurched toward the bar. "Set 'em up, Monty. . . . I'm treatin' the house."

Bottles and glasses slid across the bar into calloused palms as the crowd moved in like one man to accept the invitation. With an angry snort, Brodie swung on his heel and made for the door, gesturing to his men who trooped noisily at his back.

Sassoon's gaze sped after them. Catching the ranchman's backward glance at his former friend and employee, the gambler halted him with swiftly beckoning finger.

"Don't mind what the old fool says, Brodie," he said, joining the clustering Box B men at the door. "Ben is lit to the skies—and on the warpath because of his fancied grievance against you. His talk of throwing in with the King Buzzard is only drunken boasting—to get your goat."

"Yeah?" Brodie's tone was skeptical.

"You heard him sign on with Stenger for that cooking job," pointed out Sassoon. "Stenger will tame him down—when he gets him out to the ranch."

"You're making a mistake—hirin' the old coot," declared Brodie bluntly. He shrugged. "Ain't got time to waste discussin' him, Sassoon. Come on, boys—let's see if Slim has got that buckboard I sent him after." He nodded curtly and strode out, followed by his cold-eyed riders.

Sassoon's lip lifted in a sardonic smile. For a

moment he stared thoughtfully at the pulsating door-swings. From the hubbub of voices behind him came the bartender's complaining howl.

"Thar yuh go agin, Windy—spillin' good likker all over. Cain't yuh move 'thout knockin' down yore glass?"

Sassoon's black eyes glittered, his smile now an ugly snarl.

Chapter VI

He moved toward his private office, tapping the shoulders of Stenger and Banning as he passed the long line of men crowding the bar. They followed him, Stenger delaying to empty a final glass.

"What's Monte beefin' about?" enquired Sassoon, closing the door. "Sit down, boys. . . . Want to have a talk."

Stenger chuckled. "Monte's sore," he told the gambler. "Says Windy keeps upsettin' his drinks all over the place. Claims he don't savvy how the old maverick got so likkered up—the way he spills his drinks on the floor—'stead of in his stummick."

"Never saw Ben pie-eyed before," mused Sassoon. "Guess his row with Brodie got the best of him."

He studied Banning lazily as he spoke. "What gave you the notion to head into the Sinks, feller?"

"It was more than a notion, Sassoon," Banning answered briefly.

Stenger laughed, slapped a massive knee. "Listen to him, Joe. More than a notion, he says!" Stenger's merriment grew—he winked at his new top-hand. "It wasn't no notion, Joe," he confided. "It was a reason—a damned good reason at that." The cattleman fumbled in a pocket—drew out the crumpled reward notice. "Take a peep at this yell from Cochise, Joe."

"So that's the reason," murmured Sassoon, staring at Banning curiously. "Sheriff looking for you, eh, feller?"

The cowboy shrugged. "No denyin' what that piece of paper says," he drawled.

Sassoon scanned the list of charges. "Some tough hombre, Banning, according to what this sheriff claims. Rustler, horse thief—killer—" The gambler's eyes hardened. "What gives you the idea that this—" he tapped the reward notice— "that this is a passport into the Spanish Sinks? We have more than enough killers and rustlers running loose round here, Banning."

The fugitive shrugged. "Ask Stenger," he rejoined coolly.

"That's right, Joe," grinned the big Double S man. "Banning wasn't showin' that piece of paper to nobody. No, Joe . . . he was tied all hunky dory with Smoky's rope when I took it off of him."

Between chuckles, Stenger related the details of Smoky Kile's capture of the lone horseman in Lobo Pass.

"Sure give me a kick the way Cal beat Smoky to the draw," he concluded. "It gave me an idee, Joe. Kinda figgered Cal would make a right handy man to have on the Double S payroll—him bein' so fast with his guns—an' the King

Buzzard gang actin' so ugly. Never know when we'll have a showdown with that gang "

Stenger's voice hardened—he threw Banning a menacing glance. "Cal can do worse than play straight with us—him knowin' that a word from us to Cochise will have him in jail—with a rope danglin' for his neck. Huh, Cal?"

"Looks that way," admitted the cowboy. "Reckon I can do worse than string along with you fellers."

Sassoon nodded. "Guess you'll do, Banning. As Stenger says—we can use top-notch gun-fighters. Looks like we're in for a showdown any time with these rustlers." He gave the cowboy a friendly smile. "You go and get a bite to eat. Monte will fix you up with a sandwich."

"I'd like to fix up a feed for my horse," suggested Banning.

"No time," demurred Sassoon. "We're leaving for the Cross Knife in a few minutes."

"Cross Knife!" Stenger gave a surprised grunt. "How come you fellers ridin' to the Cross Knife?"

Sassoon told him of the promise to Anita Callahan to keep vigil at the ill-fated ranch house.

Stenger smothered an astonished oath. "That sure is a funny stunt," he puzzled, as the door closed behind Banning. "Promised the gal yuh'd sit up with the corpse, huh, Joe?" He wagged his head drunkenly. "Now ain't yuh got a good heart, Mister Sassoon!"

The gambler flung him a deadly look—went swiftly to the door and snapped the lock. Returning to the desk chair he opened a drawer and helped himself to a drink from a small cut-glass decanter.

"Sure are liberal with your whiskey, Joe," grumbled Stenger, thirsty gaze on the decanter.

"You've drunk plenty," sneered Sassoon. "One more will push you over. You go getting drunk —and the King Buzzard will be leaving you a little card—"

"Says you," muttered the cattleman, paling under his sunburn.

Sassoon relented. "Oh, hell—go to it." He slid the decanter across the desk.

"Thanks, Joe," grunted the other man. His hand trembled as he poured a drink.

Sassoon watched him satirically. "Look like you'd seen a ghost," he gibed.

"Gets my goat—talkin' about him handin' me the black feather," mumbled Stenger. He shivered —poured another drink. "Well—whatcha got on yore mind?" He eyed his elegant partner uneasily.

"Just this, Al—" Sassoon's shiny boots thudded on the floor, glittering gaze fastened on the cattleman. "You're a dumb animal. If it wasn't for me—you wouldn't be sitting pretty as part-owner of the Double S. I'm the brains back of our deals, Al—and don't you forget it."

"Whatcha drivin' at?" snarled the big man.

"Sure I'm part-owner of the Double S. That was the deal we made." He glowered resentfully. "I done plenty of the dirty work at that—earnin' title to the herd wearin' that brand—Double S—meanin' S for you—an' S for me."

The man behind the desk regarded him intently. Stenger seemed to shrink under that contemptuous scrutiny. He rapped out an oath, snatched up the decanter. Sassoon's smile grew wintry.

"Stenger," he said in a purring voice, "I've a hunch there's dogs baying on the King Buzzard's trail."

The Double S man laughed harshly—tossed the drink into his big, moist mouth. "Here's to 'em," he sneered.

"Keep on swilling that whiskey—and the dogs will get you, too," warned Sassoon. He smiled grimly. "Speaking of whiskey—your new cook—Ben Allen—is up to mischief. He's no more drunk than I am."

"Yuh're loco!" Stenger blinked. "The old rannihan is likkered to the eyes!"

"He is cold sober," insisted the gambler. "I was watching him—slopping his drinks. Didn't Monte yell about him knocking his drinks over every chance? And all that palaver about quitting the Box B!" Sassoon's expression was venomous. "Something queer is in the pot, Al. That's why I framed for you to hire him."

The cattleman grinned. "Had me guessin'—

tellin' me I'd fired ol' Tubby Jones. Figgered you'd somethin' up yore sleeve."

"I want him where we can watch him—day and night," Sassoon told him.

"I'll watch him—the crawlin' snake . . . pretending he aimed to join up with the King Buzzard." Stenger spat an oath. "I'll make buzzard's meat of him pronto."

Sassoon shook his sleek head. "Not now, you won't. I want to use him." He paused, satanic glee in his black eyes. "Windy Ben will be our unsuspecting pawn—if we play him right."

A wide grin split Stenger's red face. He got up, lurching to the door. "I get yuh," he chuckled. "Leave it to me to back yore play."

"See that you do," warned his partner grimly. He unlocked the door—drew back with a startled exclamation.

Faintly at first, they heard the quick drumming of galloping hoofs. A six-gun crashed in the street, and with a wild, piercing yell, a lone horseman tore past the Horsehead Bar.

Sassoon flung the door open and dashed down the long barroom, followed by the clamor of booted feet as the crowd surged at his heels.

The kerosene lamp in front of the saloon was no longer burning. Sassoon swore as he saw the splinters of glass on the board walk.

"Shot out my lamp!"

He peered down the dark street.

"Whoever the loon was—he's gone," said Banning at his elbow, a partly-eaten sandwich in one hand, a gun in the other.

Frightened horses snorted in the street. Here and there a few lights twinkled. They could hear men's voices—profanely conjecturing about the mysterious night rider. Asa Coons' place of business across the way was in darkness. The wondering group in front of the saloon heard his shuffling step—the tap tap of his crutches. His door opened—they could dimly see his long flat head peering out. Most of them were aware that Asa Coons slept in the rear of his loan office.

"What's going on out there?"

His astonishing voice boomed startlingly at them.

"Stenger. . . . I see you over there. . . . Was that one of your drunken riders—shooting up the town again?" Coons' deep voice was wrathful. "I warned you—I won't stand for it—"

The big voice suddenly hushed. The watchers saw him staring at something in the partly-opened door.

"Sassoon—you others—come over here." There was a curious note of fear in the banker's voice.

They streamed across the street. Coons was striking a match, cupping the little flame to throw a light on the door.

"Look," he told them, his voice shaky.

Thrust deep into the upper panel of the door

70

was a long-bladed knife, a small black feather bound to the haft.

"The King Buzzard's callin' card!" exclaimed a hoarse voice from the crowd in the street.

Coons seemed dazed, peering fearfully up and down the street. With a sudden motion he jerked the grim warning from the panel and backed into the office, closing the door.

Silently the crowd dispersed, most of the men making for their horses. Sassoon strode frowningly back to the saloon, Stenger and Banning following at his heels.

"There's Chico!" exclaimed the gambler. "Maybe he can tell us something about this knife-throwing hombre."

The old Indian halted in the lighted entrance of the saloon, sunken eyes regarding Sassoon inscrutably.

"You see him, Chico?"

"Chico see um."

"What kinda lookin' jasper was he, Chico?" Stenger asked the Indian.

Chico gestured vaguely. "No see mooch good. . . . Him ride like wind . . . gun shoot . . . make cry like um Bad Spirit. . . . Him all same black smoke in night." Chico paused, something like a toothless grin distorting his seamed face. "Him leave bad medicine." He pointed a skinny brown finger at the painted sign above the door.

There was a shrill, drunken cackle. Windy Ben Allen lurched up to Sassoon.

"Another of them callin' cards, mister—with yore name wrote on it." Ben chuckled, pointing to the knife thrust into the painted head of the horse.

Like the one left in Asa Coons' door, a black feather decorated the haft.

"Leave it there," said Sassoon, suddenly finding his tongue as Banning reached up to pluck out the knife. "Some day I'll use it on the man who put it there."

"I'm gettin' me a drink," announced Stenger unsteadily. "I'm ridin' pronto for the Double S— me an' ol' Windy—an' the boys."

"Good thing you've got your body-guard with you," sneered Sassoon. "The bogey man might get you."

He nodded grimly and turned to his horse. "Time we were riding, Banning," he muttered to the cowboy. "You and I have a date out at the Cross Knife."

Chapter VII

A mellow light spread across the eastern horizon, softening the hard glitter of the stars. Slowly a round moon pushed above a frowning dark hump that Sassoon told his companion was El Toro Peak—highest point in the San Dimas chain of mountains, enclosing the great basin of the Spanish Sinks.

The velvety darkness melted, disclosing a panorama of moon-drenched desert. Clumps of ragged mesquite loomed darkly fantastic in the shifting pools of light—and gaunt, bristling shanks of cactus and stately lance-like yucca.

They came presently to low-lying flats, matted with coarse salt grass, and clumps of tules. A few minutes' ride brought them to a river bank thicketed with salt cedars and willows, with silvery gleams of moonlit water making delicate lace of their branches. Sassoon broke the silence.

"The Big Anita," he told Banning. "Got the name from Anita Callahan's great-grandmother."

"Spreads herself wide and shallow," commented the cowboy. He eyed the shimmering, lake-like expanse before them, estimating that at least half a mile of water lay between them and the dark fringe of trees marking the opposite shore. On either side of the shallows, the river squeezed turbulently between sheer cliffs The shallows made a natural and safe ford, Banning saw. Sassoon quickly disabused him.

"A death trap," he said. He indicated two huge black cottonwood trees standing about fifteen yards apart. "Those old cottonwoods are the markers for this side—lay a course of good hard gravel bank straight for that gap in the cedar brakes on the other side. Keep to that gravel bar and you can ride across without wetting your stirrups. Get careless—and you'll be fighting quicksand—with the odds a thousand to one against you."

"Not so good for cattle," surmised the cowboy shrewdly.

"There's a story about that," said Sassoon, "almost a legend, you'd call it—about when Don Mike made a drive of Cross Knife cattle—some five thousand head—and lost half of 'em in the suck-holes. Callahan's Crossing, they call it since then." Sassoon's smile was malicious, as though the incident of that fatal crossing pleased him. "That was a long time ago. Callahan had just become Don José Pinzon's son-in-law and didn't know much about the country."

Sassoon's dark face seemed suddenly malignant under the pouring moonlight. Banning looked at him curiously.

"Listened to a gringo and lost his birthright," muttered Sassoon, somber gaze on the silvery spread of water. "Before the Mexican War, the Pinzon holdings took in some four thousand square miles—running from El Toro Peak to below the Rio Grande. More than six million acres—Pinzon land by royal grant from a king of Spain since 1590."

Again that stark hate flickered in the gambler's eyes. His voice shook.

"It was a crime. For over three centuries scores of thousands of cattle carried the crossed daggers of the Pinzons on their hides—and would today—but for the young Irish Callahan marrying Anita Pinzon and insisting they remain on the American side of the new border after the Treaty of Guadalupe Hidalgo. Gave up the Pinzon birthright so that Callahan's offspring would be Americans." He gestured contemptuously. "And now the Cross Knife takes in less than eight hundred square miles—less than half a million acres."

"Some ranch at that," commented Banning. "I'd say this Don Mike played his cards good. Kept the best of the water-shed. And maybe those revolutions would have trimmed the old royal grant a lot worse if he'd stayed below the border—gone Mex. Lot of that stuff down there is no-count desert at that."

"Maybe so," agreed Sassoon. "There's water enough—enough for the whole of the Spanish Sinks. The Don Mikes have always hogged it."

They went splashing into the shallows, riding closely side by side. Leaving the Big Anita they kept the horses to a steady trot. The hills closed in, and suddenly the ancient Cross Knife hacienda lay before them, set deeply back in a grove of tall trees. Sassoon jerked his black gelding to a halt.

"That's queer!" His voice was surprised. "No lights showing!"

The lifeless windows of the house stared at them through the moon-drenched trees. It was a low rambling building, with weathered grayish-red walls that could be softly colorful in the bright sunshine of day, but now bulking with sinister menace under the phantom light of the moon.

Beyond the trees loomed the darker outlines of barns and stables, from which swept a maze of corrals, and set on a low hill to the right of the house, a tiny belfried chapel, with a cross vaguely limned against the night sky.

High, vine-covered walls enclosed a garden behind the chapel—the ancient burial grounds of the Pinzons and the Callahans, Banning decided.

The air was heavy with the cloying sweet of honeysuckle, mingling with the delicate perfume of rose and jasmine. The sunlight of day would bring the droning of bees in the flowers, and the twitter and song of birds in the trees. There was no stirring of life now. Banning spoke, vaguely oppressed by the foreboding stillness.

"Makes me feel sort of creepy," he confessed. "I'll be seeing spooks—if we sit here starin' at that old house."

They rode forward, leaving the road, pushing across the cropped grass under the trees to the front of the house. Sassoon swung from his saddle and went up the steps to the massive door, his tread sending hollow echoes down the long, brick-paved gallery.

"The girl told us that Don Mike was lying here in the entrance," he reminded the cowboy in a puzzled voice. "She tried to drag him inside—but he was too heavy. She left him lying here—the door wide open—"

"I'd say that proves Doc Spicer is somewhere round," Banning commented. "There's no dead man lying there now—and the door is shut."

"He'd have a light burning," Sassoon pointed out. "Something queer—about this." He gave the brass door handle a shake. "Locked on the inside —bolted," he added.

Fastened to the wall, close to the door, was an old-fashioned bell-pull. He reached up and gave it a vigorous jerk. A jangling of bells from somewhere in the house reached them, startlingly loud in the dead silence of the night. They listened tensely. The jangling bells hushed.

"Give him a yell," suggested Banning.

"No use in that," grumbled Sassoon. He went back to his horse. "Let's ride round to the corrals and see if we can spot Doc Spicer's horse. Always rides a paint mare—and takes an old Piute along to carry his bag and tend to the horse."

They rode across the grass, lanced with moonlight and shadows, swinging into the road that led to the corrals. The trees dropped behind and in a few moments they were threading the network of fences surrounding the rancho stables. Banning's bay stallion suddenly snorted.

"Smells something he don't like," observed the cowboy.

"Smells blood," Sassoon said grimly. His own horse snorted, reared. With a muttered curse, the gambler spurred the frightened animal up to the gate where Banning had halted the stallion. The cowboy was staring down at something sprawled in the dust against the open gate.

"That'll be one of the Cross Knife riders." Banning gestured at the pitiful, crumpled body of the dead man.

"There's more of 'em lying round," returned Sassoon, reining his horse savagely. "Go on, man—get through that gate—before this fool goes crazy!"

Ears twitching nervously, the big stallion trotted into the corral, past the earthly remains of what was once a Cross Knife cowboy. There was a plunging of hoofs behind. Sassoon's snorting horse bolted by, leaping high over another shapeless heap suddenly appearing in its path.

Snorting and bucking, the terrified black swung in a mad dash around the big enclosure.

Banning reached the stable and slid from his saddle, gaze following the other man battling with the frenzied horse. For the first time he saw the suave Sassoon bereft of his imperturbable calm. Tigerish ferocity distorted the man's face. Using quirt and spur he forced the maddened animal to the stable doors and flung himself from the saddle. With a saturnine grin at the cowboy, he led the trembling black into the dark interior.

Banning followed with the stallion, turning into an empty stall. From the adjoining stall came more snorts from the black horse—a startled oath from Sassoon.

"Another dead man," he called out. "Can't take a step without falling over dead men."

He led the gelding into another stall. From the darker end of the stable came a soft nicker.

"Maybe that's the doc's paint mare," called Banning. He was pulling hay from the rack, stuffing it into the manger.

He heard Sassoon stumbling down the runway. A match flared.

"It's the paint mare," came his voice. "The Indian's bronc is here, too. . . . Both of 'em saddled."

Sassoon came stumbling back, rejoining his companion who was bending over the silent form huddled against the manger of the empty stalk.

Sassoon lit another match and glanced at the staring-eyed face.

"It's Buck Conley," he told Banning.

The match flickered out, but not before they glimpsed something sticking in the neckband of the dead man's shirt.

"Did you see it?" Banning's voice was hard. "Did you see it, Sassoon? The black feather!" He bent down. "Let's carry him out. . . . Keeps the horses nervous—him lying here."

They carried the remains of poor Buck Conley out and put him gently down against the corral fence.

"That makes three of 'em," Banning said. "The other two we saw will be Bert and Pete—the boys Clem Sanders sent in from Toro Lake with this Buck Conley hombre." He pushed back his Stetson and looked at Sassoon.

"Queer—Doc Spicer leaving 'em here like dead dogs," he puzzled.

"Not so queer as where Doc Spicer is," returned the other man curtly. "Old fool—playing tricks like this!"

"Wouldn't go off and leave his bronc, would he?"

"Don't seem reasonable he would," grunted Sassoon. "Well—let's take a look at the house."

Banning gestured at the dead man lying in the middle of the corral. "Let's tote him over to the fence," he suggested.

"Let him lie," came the callous rejoinder. "It's Don Mike we came to look after."

He moved on. Banning glared indignantly, then muttering under his breath he gathered the lifeless cowboy in his arms and followed.

Sassoon was waiting as he came to the gate with his burden and placed it against the fence.

"Well," drawled the gambler, "if that's the way you feel about it—" He stooped over the crumpled form lying against the gate. "Bronco Pete," he said as he carried the dead man to the fence and laid him down by the side of the other Cross Knife man. "An old timer on the Cross Knife," he added, glancing at the still face. "Worked a lot of Cross Knife cows in his time."

He gave Banning a friendly slap on the back. "You're sure tender-hearted for an outlaw," he jeered.

The tall cowboy shrugged. "You're not so hard yourself, Sassoon," he retorted.

They moved through the gate, approaching the house from the rear. It loomed before them, ghostly-gray against the dark blur of trees. Moonshine glanced sullen leaden gleams from a window. A wind sprang up—went softly moaning through the trees.

Chapter VIII

A narrow corridor, paved with worn red bricks, led them into a patio, with a gallery running round the four sides of the building. Sassoon, evidently familiar with his surroundings, pointed out the servants' quarters. The kitchen door was open. They struck matches and looked in. What they saw left them both pale.

"The cook," muttered Sassoon, closing the door. "The boy you saw with the knife in him was Anita's groom."

"The cowards!" Banning's gray eyes blazed. "What would they go and kill an old woman for—and that Indian kid?"

"Recognized some of the gang," surmised Sassoon. "It was kill them or be exposed."

"Proves that the members of the gang are not strangers in the Sinks," said Banning.

They stared across the patio at the main wing. The big hall door was wide open, pale moonlight filtering through a small oriole window above the front entrance at the farther end of the passage.

Tensely the two men eyed that funnel of ghostly gray light, ears alert for some stirring of life within those old walls. Only the moaning of the wind came to them—and the soft splashing of a little fountain in the middle of the walled garden.

"Don't often see a place like this on a cowranch," observed Banning. "Like some old hacienda down below the border."

"Been here a long time," Sassoon told him. "More than a hundred and fifty years since Pinzon peons quarried the red sandstone that went into those walls."

Their high-heeled boots clattered along the walk—rough-hewn slabs of stone worn smooth by the years, green edgings of grass growing in the cracks.

"Seems to me that Doc Spicer—or his Indian, would hear us out here," puzzled the cowboy. "How do you figure it, Sassoon?"

"Ask me another," growled the gambler.

He strode into the gloomy hall. Banning followed, eyes wary. Suspended from the ceiling was an oil lamp in a handsome wrought-iron frame. He put a match to the wick, eyeing around curiously as the soft lamplight flooded the hall.

He saw richly-paneled walls of blackened oak, lined with portraits of stately caballeros and lovely-eyed señoras and señoritas.

"Meet the Pinzons," introduced Sassoon. He gestured at a large canvas hung over the wide entrance to the living-room. "The gentleman wearing a steel breast-plate and sword is Don José de Pinzon, soldier of fortune in the army of Cortez—and first lord of the Cross Knife Rancho by royal grant from his king."

There was a curiously eager expression in Banning's gray eyes as he studied the bold, predatory face staring at him from the wall.

"The old conquistador himself, huh? Looks like one fightin' hombre."

He shifted his gaze to a lovely dark-eyed face smiling from the opposite wall. He stared, fascinated. The resemblance to Anita Callahan was startling.

"Not hard to guess who *she* is, eh, Banning?" remarked Sassoon.

"No—not hard to guess who she is," muttered the cowboy. His face was oddly pale. "The Callahan girl could have doubled for that—"

"Her great-grandmother," drawled Sassoon. "The Anita Pinzon who became the mother of Don Mike Callahan. The miniature next to her is the gringo husband—first of the Cross Knife Callahans—painted by the fair Anita herself."

Sassoon's eyes narrowed. "What's the matter, Banning? Seen a ghost?"

The cowboy looked round from the miniature of the first Don Mike Callahan. "Not ghosts—" he answered in a strained voice. "Was kind of dreaming—kind of picturing him—" He nodded at the miniature—"when he came ridin' here to the Cross Knife—a wild, fightin' young Irishman —making love to a daughter of the dons." Banning glanced at the steady gray eyes in the miniature. "Didn't they have two sons, Sassoon—twins?"

"Why do you ask?" Sassoon gave him a sharp glance.

"Seems I've heard some story about another son bein' stolen by raidin' Indians—or Mexicans," said Banning. "Maybe it's just one of those old border tales that float round. He'd be the Callahan girl's great-uncle if he were alive."

"There is some truth in the story," admitted Sassoon indifferently. "There was a twin brother —but he didn't live long enough to count—just a few days."

The cowboy stared at him steadily. "Just a few days—Sassoon? Is that right?"

"Only know what I've heard," Sassoon shrugged. "You seem sort of interested, Banning."

"What became of Anita Callahan's own dad?" queried the cowboy, ignoring the remark. "He'd have been the third Don Mike."

"He was killed by rustlers," Sassoon told him. "Anita was about a week old. . . . The shock killed her mother." Sassoon was eyeing the young man suspiciously. "Any more questions, mister?"

Banning stared around the great hall, drew in a long breath. "No more Don Mike Callahans," he muttered. "Only a girl—one girl—left."

"Correct, mister," said Sassoon softly. His black eyes glittered. "No more Don Mikes—only a dead one—lying somewhere in this old house." He pointed at a pair of silver candlesticks.

"Light 'em, Banning. . . . We'll take a look round the place."

The cowboy lighted the candles and each took one. Banning spoke again, his tone surprised.

"That's funny!" He pointed at a blue and gold portiere draping one side of the living-room entrance. "The one on the other side is missing!"

"More mystery!" ejaculated Sassoon in an astonished voice. "And not missing long! Why, feller—that drape's been taken down only a little while ago. . . . See—you can tell by the dust marks." He shrugged. "Well—let's have a look-see."

Beginning with the living-room, they searched the house, even peering into a dainty bedroom they instinctively guessed was the Callahan girl's own. The search left them baffled, but convinced that the late Don Mike was not in the halls of his ancestors. Nor could they materialize the missing Doc Spicer and his Indian servant.

"If it weren't for those sure-dead waddies out there in the corral—and those bloodstains there by the hall door, I'd say we've been dreaming—and call it a day," declared Banning. He slid his candlestick back on the hall table. "Maybe Don Mike wasn't dead—when the doc got here," he suggested. "Maybe the doc and the Indian took him off some place . . . scared of the King Buzzard gang coming back—or something—"

"They wouldn't leave their horses in the stable," pointed out Sassoon. "You can't explain things that way, Banning."

Banning gave him a warning look. "Horses coming," he said softly. His hand darted to the lamp, jerking the burner chain, snuffing the wick to a smoking red fringe. Moonlight again stole in through the little oriole window, reaching vague, gray fingers through the blackness, touching the whites of Sassoon's eyes.

"Doc Spicer," surmised the latter uneasily.

"Too many horses," argued the cowboy. He went noiselessly to the patio door.

Sassoon followed him out. Hugging the shadows of the deep gallery, the two men waited, listening to the muffled thuds approaching across the thick turf under the trees.

"Coming round the right wing of the *casa*," muttered Banning. "The dining room windows will give us a look at 'em." He slid silent as a wraith into the dark hall, Sassoon at his heels.

The curtains were drawn in the dining room, shutting out the moonlight, forcing them to stumble cautiously through inky darkness. Sassoon's spur tangled with some unseen object. Muttering a curse, he jerked violently, sprawling with a thud on the floor as the spur tore loose. There was a loud crash of breaking glass, followed by a girl's startled cry outside.

"What the devil—!" It was Sassoon's astonished

voice somewhere in the darkness. He swore softly, struggled to his feet.

Startled by the crash—the frightened cry of the girl, Banning had come to a halt in the middle of the room. Sassoon came groping up to him.

"Caught my foot on that damned bearskin . . . fell into a glass door—" His hand clutched the cowboy's arm. "Did you hear it—that scream?" Sassoon's voice was incredulous. "It was the Callahan girl!"

The riders had evidently halted. Not a sound came from the night outside. The two men stared at each other wonderingly. Suddenly the silence was broken by a man's deep voice, bewildered, suspicious—loudly demanding.

"What's goin' on in there? . . . Sassoon—Banning? Is that you fellers in the house?"

"Brodie!" exclaimed the cowboy in a relieved tone.

He stumbled to a window, jerked aside the heavy curtain and tugged the French window open. Bright moonlight lay in pools on the grass, but the riders remained invisible, merged in the deep shadows of tree and bush. Sassoon joined him. There was a stirring in the shadows. A horseman rode into the revealing moonlight.

"That you, Sassoon—there in the window?" His voice was suspicious. "Where's your lights?"

"Didn't know who it was riding in," answered Sassoon, stepping through the window. "Wasn't taking chances, Brodie. . . . Might have been the gang. What brings you and Miss Callahan here?" Sassoon's tone was puzzled.

Vague shapes stirred in the deep shadows under the trees, resolving into Anita Callahan and Clem Sanders. Behind them rode a girl unknown to Banning, and—to his astonishment—the swarthy Double S man—Smoky Kile.

"Anita couldn't stand it—being over at the Box B—and her grandfather lyin' here," Brodie told them. "Clem figgered his job was here—him being foreman of the Cross Knife. His shoulder ain't hurt as bad as we thought." Brodie climbed from his horse. "Nell was bound to come along with us. . . . Says Anita needs her at a time like this." He looked over his shoulder at Smoky Kile. "Young feller—you come hornin' into this party—now you can be useful stablin' the broncs. Come on girls—and you, Clem." He strode to the French window. "Give us a light— one of you men. . . . We're comin' through the window."

A match flamed in Banning's hand. He turned quickly away—saw a silver candelabra on the dining table. He touched his match to the candles, and into their soft aureole stepped Anita and her friends.

"Where—where is he?"

She looked at Banning with grief-stricken eyes. He hesitated, darted a worried glance at Sassoon who was taking his time closing and locking the French window.

"Well, young feller?" Brodie spoke up impatiently. "Heard her—didn't you?"

"That's what is puzzling Sassoon and me," reluctantly answered the cowboy.

They stared at him, bewildered. Sassoon came up. Anita whirled on him.

"What does he mean? Where's grandfather, Mr. Sassoon?"

"We don't know, Anita." Sassoon's voice was troubled. "Banning and I rode out here as we promised—but Don Mike isn't here . . . at least not in the house. We've searched every room."

"Not—not here?" she faltered. "I—I don't understand." She began to tremble. Nell Brodie, a wholesome-looking girl with a curly bob of corn-colored hair, slipped a comforting arm round her.

The Box B man and Clem Sanders exchanged glances. The latter spoke bluntly.

"That's a queer story, Sassoon." He looked at Brodie. "Thought you sent Doc Spicer out here, Jim."

"Mr. Coons sent him," corrected Anita in a faint voice.

"That's right," corroborated Brodie. "Spicer was ridin' off—when I rode into town. . . . Him and his Indian. Wasn't 'til then I heard the news about the raid." He eyed Sassoon and Banning

90

suspiciously. "Don't mean to say Doc Spicer ain't here?"

"He's been here—by the signs," broke in Banning. "His mare is in the barn—and the Indian's bronc—at least Sassoon claims they are."

The gambler nodded. "That's right. Spicer's been here—but he's not here now—no more than Don Mike is. How do you figure it out, Brodie?"

"I don't figure it out," confessed the big ranchman. He seemed dazed, unable to cope with the mystery.

"Can't *you* think of some explanation—some place to look," implored Anita, turning her golden brown eyes on Banning.

He sensed that for some reason, she had instinctively appealed to him rather than to Sassoon—or even her own foreman. He answered slowly.

"I'd say the answer is this Doc Spicer, Miss Callahan. Find him—and we'll know what's been happening here—" He paused, frowning thoughtfully at Sassoon. "You know Doc Spicer right well, don't you, Sassoon? Better than any of us. Livin' in town—you and Doc Spicer see a lot of each other, I reckon."

Sassoon shrugged. "Deducing what, mister?"

"Drops in at your Horsehead Bar a lot—maybe. . . . Likes his little snort once in a while, eh, Sassoon?"

A curious expression crept into the saloon

91

man's black eyes, as though Banning's last question had touched off a startling train of thought. He looked at Anita.

"Don Mike had a cellar, I suppose, Anita?" he asked her.

"You mean—liquor?" She nodded. "He always made a lot of wine every year . . . thought a lot of the old vineyard and was proud of his wines." Her voice was mystified. "Why do you ask?"

Sassoon's gaze went to the cowboy. "You struck a lead, mister. Doc Spicer was a great surgeon—until liquor took hold of him. That's why he ended up in San Carlos. A good doc when he's sober—but one worthless human when he's soused—and that is most of the time."

"Oh, you mean—"

Anita's voice was horrified.

"Exactly," said Sassoon. "Doc Spicer got here all right—tapped the cellar—got drunk—his Indian, too—then went and hid Don Mike somewhere."

"Might be a good idea to have a look at this cellar," suggested Banning.

"We'll need a lantern," said Anita. "The wine room is in the old wing."

She found one in the hall closet and they all trooped out to the patio, Banning carrying the lantern.

The chain dangling on the wine room door told them it was not locked. Banning swung it open and stepped inside, followed by Brodie and Sassoon. The others, waiting outside, heard a surprised grunt from Brodie—muttered exclamations, and presently the three men hurried out of the vault-like room. From their baffled looks it was plain that the mystery had deepened. Anita's eyes questioned Banning. He shook his head.

"No luck," he said briefly.

"But you—you did find something!" she insisted. "You know you did!"

"Just the Indian," Brodie told her. "Drunk himself senseless. No sign of Doc Spicer—nor your grandpa."

There was a stunned silence. From the corrals came the sound of crunching boots, and Smoky Kile clattered through the corridor into the patio. He halted, staring wonderingly at the little group in front of the wine room. Sassoon went to him and they stood for a moment in low-voiced conference.

Banning looked at Anita. "Any other place we might look?" he asked her. "Finding the Indian in there proves we've struck a warm trail."

She shook her head helplessly.

"You're all worn out!" cried Nell Brodie. She flung her arms round the drooping little figure. "Honey—you come back to the house and go to bed!"

"I can't, Nell," protested the girl. "I just couldn't—not until I know where he is!"

Sassoon rejoined them, Smoky Kile at his heels. The latter gave Clem Sanders a sour glance as he observed the Cross Knife foreman holding hands with the fair-haired Brodie girl. Throwing Banning a grim nod of recognition, the Double S man stamped into the wine room.

"Told Smoky to haul him out to the corral," explained Sassoon as Kile staggered out with the sleeping Piute in his arms.

Anita gave the drunken Indian a shuddering glance. The cowboy grinned at them, boot heels loudly clipping the corridor stones as he hurried past with his burden.

"And that's that," murmured Sassoon. He gave Banning a sardonic look. "Leaving us where—mister detective—"

"Listen!" interrupted Anita. She clutched Banning's arm. "Listen—I hear bells—bells!"

Chapter IX

Faintly at first, the sound came to them through the night—the pealing of bells, swelling to solemn, measured tolling for the dead. Anita's fingers tightened on Banning's arm.

"The chapel bells!" she said in a low, amazed voice. "What does it mean?"

She went with flying feet across the patio. They hurried after her into the hall still softly aglow with candle light. Banning overtook her at the massive front door.

"Quick!" she gasped, fumbling at the stiff, heavy bolts.

He jerked at the bolts, flung the door open. She fled past him, down a path winding under the trees. Again he overtook her as she paused at the Gothic doors set deep in the ancient walls of the little church. The pealing bells had hushed, but a pale finger of light came from between the partly-opened doors and lay across the worn stones of the wide corridor steps. Sassoon and the others came on hurrying feet, the noise of their approach suddenly silenced as amazed eyes saw the candle gleam thinly ribboning through the doors.

Banning looked at the girl by his side. Again he sensed that unspoken appeal. She was trembling, her eyes dark pools in the white oval of her face. He sprang up the old stone steps and vanished into the gloom of the chapel. Almost instantly the breathless group saw his tall figure reappear.

"Well—?" Sassoon's voice, nervous, rasping, broke the silence.

"He's in there," said Banning in a hushed, awed voice. "Don Mike is in there—" He gestured at the gaping doors.

There was a gasp from Anita. Brushing aside Sassoon's detaining hand, she darted up the steps and ran inside.

"Wait!" Banning spoke in the same curiously hushed tone as the others crowded quickly up. "Give her a minute—alone in there—with him!"

"Wait nothing!" Sassoon eyed him furiously. "Men on the Double S payroll don't give orders to me, fellow." He strode to the tall doors of weathered oak and bronze brought from old Spain by a long-gone Pinzon. Banning's arm, like a steel-hard bar, pressed him back.

"You don't understand, Sassoon. Don Mike is in there—lying on a sort of bier in front of the altar, with candles burning. Lying there—like all the other Cross Knife dons that have gone before him. He's the last of them—and she's his granddaughter. She'll want to say a prayer for him—kneelin' by his side."

"Reckon you are right, Banning," muttered Sassoon, falling back. His dark skin had taken on a curious pallor. "It's a sacred moment for—for her." He crossed himself.

The minutes went by. The girl did not reappear. Brodie spoke, voice uneasy. "Let's go in, folks. We've given her time enough."

Silent, they trailed in behind him, startled eyes reaching down the dim aisle to the slim young girl kneeling by the bier at the foot of the chancel steps.

The still remains of the slain owner of the Cross Knife Rancho lay on a blue and gold brocade draped over rough planks supported by up-ended boxes. Candles burned on either side of the improvised bier, and on the altar. Banning recognized the blue and gold drape as the one missing from the door in the great hall.

As if sensing their wondering gaze, the girl slowly rose and faced them, hands fluttering to her breast in a summoning gesture. They gathered around, staring in silent bewilderment at the body of the last of the Don Mike Callahans. There was majestic dignity in the calm repose of the face strongly marked by the haughty Pinzon features. It was in the huge frame, the mighty-thewed limbs, and the touch of red in white hair and patriarchial beard, that Banning saw the strain of the fighting Callahans. His gaze went to the granddaughter. She was speaking in a low, bewildered voice.

"I—I can't understand it! Who has done this for him—carried him here—like this?"

From somewhere out of the surrounding gloom a curious little sound reached Banning, a sound as yet apparently unnoticed by the others, a scarcely audible, cadenced rasping noise that in a flash solved the mystery—a solution so bizarre that he detested the thought of disclosing it to the already over-strung girl. He wanted desperately to get her away. Too late he saw her dark eyes dilate—the slim body go tense.

There was no mistaking the nature of the sound that rhythmically breathed through the silence in the little chapel. Anita stifled an astonished exclamation.

"Listen!" she whispered. "There's a man here asleep—snoring!"

"Doc Spicer," said Banning.

She gave him an amazed glance.

"Easy to guess what's happened," went on Banning. He looked at Sassoon.

"That's Doc Spicer for you," sneered the tall gambler. "Always spectacular—sentimental, when he's drunk—"

"I don't care if he *is* drunk!" interrupted Anita indignantly. "It was nice of him—to do this—" Her voice died away, startled gaze leaping to a narrow door leading into the belfry.

Framed in the entrance stood a balloon-stomached little man, teetering precariously on thin, spindly legs. Massive head was thatched with a shock of iron-gray hair, under which glistened a broad pink face. He addressed them with drunken solemnity.

"I'm afraid I have been remiss in my vigil. Morpheus lured me from a sacred duty, alas."

"You mean you let Bacchus lure you, don't you, Doc?" jeered Sassoon.

Anita darted the saloon man a furious look. "I'm sure Doctor Spicer has been very kind," she began.

"Not at all," interrupted the doctor. "Only decent thing to do." He tottered toward them, grasping the back of a pew. "Should not have taken so much wine—but was overcome by the—the horror of it all. . . . My old friend—lying there in his blood—his people slain like dogs. I found myself sick—sick!" Dr. Spicer's thin, reedy voice was a despairing shriek. "You—Sassoon! What means your presence here—*here?*" The broad pink face twitched, and with a strangled cry the fat little doctor crumpled to the floor by the side of the bier.

"Poor old man!" exclaimed Anita sorrowfully. "It was too much for him! I don't blame him!" Again she instinctively turned to Banning. "We must get him to the house. He is really ill."

"You're coining, too," declared Brodie. "Nell—you and Clem take her back. Get her to bed." He looked at Banning. "All right, feller—let's tote this jasper out of here." He bent down to the limp figure on the floor.

"That's right, Anita," put in Sassoon. "You run along and get some rest. I'll stay here with Don Mike."

Reluctantly she went out with Nell and Clem. Brodie and Banning took up the senseless doctor. Banning said:

"The doc seemed some upset—seeing you here, Sassoon."

"Why shouldn't he—getting drunk on the job?" frigidly answered the gambler. He glanced angrily at the tall cowboy. "Seems to me you're mighty officious, Banning. Don't forget who you are and let Miss Callahan go to your head," he added pointedly.

"Meanin' what?" demanded Banning, reddening.

"Figure it out for yourself," sneered Sassoon. "Stenger hired you to work for the Double S—but I'm firing you if you talk too loud round me, cowboy."

"This ain't no time to start an argument," complained Brodie. "Get goin', Banning."

They moved down the aisle with their burden, Sassoon watching, a speculative glitter in his black eyes. Mechanically he extracted a cigarette from his silver case, his gaze returning to the giant frame of the slain Don Mike lying so still on the blue and gold brocade. The sight seemed to unnerve him. Muttering an imprecation he went swiftly out to the stone corridor. A match flamed in his fingers, touched the cigarette, and leaning against the massive chapel door, he thoughtfully watched Brodie and Banning as they vanished into the darkness under the trees with the unconscious Doc Spicer.

Chapter X

"Nell's puttin' her to bed," Clem Sanders told Brodie as the latter and Banning entered the hall with their burden. "She says for you to put the doc in that spare room down the patio . . . wants you to make sure he's fixed up comfortable."

The young Cross Knife foreman seemed remarkably cheerful, considering his recently wounded arm which he now carried in a sling. Banning shrewdly suspected that Brodie's pretty blonde daughter had more than a little to do with Clem's pleasant mood.

"Lead the way, mister," he grinned. "Our friend Doc is gettin' heavy on the arms."

They followed the foreman through the hall and went clattering down the patio corridor to a room in the end wing. A lamp was burning, the windows open to the cooling night air. One of the windows looked out on the patio—the other opened to the grove of trees outside the *casa* walls.

"Reckon he's coming out of his faint," said Banning as they placed Spicer on the bed. "Sure was queer—the way he keeled over back there in the chapel," he added.

"Huh!" snorted Brodie; "drunk wine enough to make any man keel over." He looked round as boots clattered across the patio. "That you, Smoky? What you do with the old Piute?"

"Left him snorin' his haid off back in a strawpile," the Double S man told them from the doorway. "Where's Nell?" he added, darting a jealous glance at Clem Sanders.

"You're wastin' your time, Kile," answered the latter thinly. "Might as well be on your way, mister."

"I ride when I git ready to ride," retorted the swart-faced cowboy belligerently. "Who do yuh think yuh are—givin' me orders?"

"I'm foreman of this ranch, Kile—and I'm tellin' you that you ain't welcome at the Cross Knife."

"I come here with Nell—an' her dad," reminded Smoky furiously.

"No more of that fightin' talk," growled Nell's father. He glowered at the Double S man. "And keep your hand away from your gun, Smoky. Wait for Clem's shootin' arm to mend up before you start that sort of play." Looking at Clem, he added quietly, "Reckon it's up to Nell to say if she wants Smoky to be on his way, young man."

"The doc's coming out of it," broke in Banning's voice. "Less noise there, boys."

The fat man groaned, sat up with an effort, put a shaking hand to his leonine head. "Gosh— gimme a drink—somebody!" he gasped.

"Here yuh are, Doc." Smoky Kile whipped a

flask from hip-pocket and tendered it with a knowing grin at the others. "Some of the hair of the dog that bit yuh, Doc."

"U—ugh!" Doc Spicer shuddered, snatched at the flask. "Just a swallow," he apologized with an attempt at professional dignity. He gulped noisily, made a wry face and handed the flask back to Kile. "Let me see," he rambled, "I was—was—ah—yes—I—" He broke off, horror filling his eyes. "It is too fiendish!" he suddenly screamed, "too utterly diabolical—this ruthless killing! I can't hold my silence! I must tell you—tell you—" He paused, trembling, perspiration beading broad pink face.

"Yes," encouraged Banning, "what is it you want to tell us, Doc?"

"The ol' coot has the willies—he's off his haid," muttered Smoky Kile uneasily. He drew back from the bed, sudden fear in his eyes, pausing as a girl's indignant voice echoed down the corridor.

"Dad! Can't you keep him quiet? That yelling has Anita all upset again!"

"It's all right, Nell. The doc is just some nervous," answered Brodie. He eyed Spicer curiously. "Go on, Doc. You was sayin' something about these killin's—"

"I tell yuh—he's crazy," repeated Kile. "Reckon I'll be goin'."

"Going where?" demanded Clem Sanders

suspiciously. "If you think you're goin' to sneak out to Nell—you've got another think comin'!"

"Shut up, Clem," growled the Box B owner. He swung an angry face at Kile. "Smoky—you stay in this room. Nell ain't wantin' you sparkin' round her to-night. All right, Doc. . . . Talk up. You got me plumb curious. And keep your voice down—or you'll get Anita throwin' hysterics."

"Let me up," muttered Spicer. "Want some air." He slid from the bed and lurched to the window fronting the grove of trees.

The Box B cattleman stared at the pudgy doctor intently. Banning saw that he was nervously taut, seething with impatience—and ugly suspicions, as was Clem Sanders, keeping a watchful eye on the reluctant Smoky Kile sullenly waiting near the door.

"Spicer," said Brodie in an ominous, threatening voice, "you was talkin' about these killin's. You've said too much—or too little—" The big cattleman's voice shook with suppressed fury. "Talk some more, Spicer. Is it this murderin' devil we call the King Buzzard—you aim to name?"

The doctor slowly turned from the window and faced them. His big face was ghastly, blotched with terror. He said huskily:

"Brodie—it may mean the black feather for me—cost me my life—but I'm willing to tell what I know—if it will clean out this horror from the Spanish Sinks. Yes—I am one of the few who know the identity of the monster we call the King Buzzard. You'll be astonished, Brodie. It's too unbelievable—a horrible joke on all of you. The King Buzzard is—is—" The crash of a six-gun blasted the name from Doc Spicer's tongue. His pudgy body jerked convulsively, and with a curious choking cough he toppled in a sprawling heap to the floor.

For a moment they stared in stunned silence, then with a furious exclamation, Brodie bent over the twitching body. "He's gone," he muttered in a bitter, disappointed tone. "That slug tore the spine out of him!"

"The killer was back in those trees," said Banning, eyeing the open window. Drawing his gun he rushed from the room, followed by the others.

Light feet pattered down the corridor—Nell Brodie and Anita, the latter with an old-rose wrap drawn over her night-dress, ankles gleaming smoothly white above blue satin mules. She halted abruptly, dark, alarmed eyes bringing Banning to a standstill.

"What is it? Who's been shot?" Her voice was panicky.

"Doc Spicer," he told her curtly, and sped across the patio to the outer gate.

Behind him he heard Brodie's excited voice. "Smoky—you go with Banning. I'm headin' for the front through the hall. Clem—you stay with the girls."

106

Gun in hand, Banning tore through the gate, the Double S man pounding noisily behind. The moon had dipped below the western wall of hills, leaving the grove of trees engulfed in dense blackness.

"Cain't see a thing!" gasped Smoky. He stumbled, lurched against Banning. The impact threw them both off their feet and they went sprawling into a bush. Banning felt a crash against his head. The blow left him in a daze. Frantically he fought off the billowing void reaching out to engulf him. Somewhere in the bushes close by he vaguely sensed Smoky Kile, cursing luridly as he extricated himself from clutching thorns. He sat up, dizzy, conscious of other sounds—the quick clumping of booted feet—a man's excited voice —Brodie's voice.

"That you, Sassoon?"

"What's wrong at the house?" It was Sassoon's voice. "Thought I heard a gunshot, Brodie?"

"Another killin'," came Brodie's voice. "Doc Spicer—this time. Somebody out here in the woods gunned him through the window."

"The hell you say!" Sassoon's voice was shocked.

"Where was you, Sassoon—when you heard the shootin'?" queried the Box B cattleman suspiciously.

"Where do you suppose?" rejoined the gambler tartly. "Was back there in the chapel—with the body. Heard the shot and come runnin'."

"You didn't see nothin', Sassoon?"

"Too dark," grumbled the gambler. "Heard a lot of noise in the bushes over there to the left. Sounded like a man beatin' it away fast."

There was an excited exclamation from Brodie and again the quick crunching of running feet. Banning's head was clearing. He got to his feet, saw Smoky Kile grinning at him.

"Yuh sure took a nasty crack agin' that tree stump, mister," he said. His voice rose warningly. "Careful there, fellers! It's me an' Banning—here in the brush!"

Brodie and Sassoon panted up, drawn guns in hands. Smoky grinned at them.

"Me an' Banning sort of tangled our laigs an' took a spill. Banning went an' busted his haid on that stump. Kinda knocked him silly."

Sassoon swore softly. "Reckon that settles it, Brodie. Whoever pulled off that killin' made a clean getaway."

Brodie grunted like an angry bear, eyes fixed on Banning. "Hurt bad, son?"

The cowboy shook his head, staring thoughtfully at Smoky Kile, the tips of his exploring fingers wet from the gash in his scalp. "Sure was a hard old stump," he told them ruefully.

Sassoon said sadly, "So poor old Doc is dead! What do you make of it, Brodie? Who do you suppose bumped him off?"

"The first question is easy," Brodie told him.

108

"Spicer was wise to the King Buzzard . . . was about to spill his name to us when he was shot. Who did the killin' is one more mystery. Must have been listenin' under the window."

Sassoon's gaze shifted to Smoky Kile. "Where'd you leave that Piute, Smoky?"

"Dumped him in a straw stack. What about it?"

"There's your answer, Brodie." Conviction was in Sassoon's voice. "You won't find that Piute where Smoky left him."

"You mean—" Brodie's snort was skeptical. "You mean the Indian done it?"

"You've said it," declared Sassoon. "The Piute killed Doc Spicer sure as we're standing here. Must have sneaked up to the window—heard the talk—and shut the doc's mouth for keeps."

"Come on, fellers!" Brodie plunged through the darkness in the direction of the corral.

"One moment, boys," rasped Sassoon. "Smoky —guess you know Banning's been hired to ride for the Double S—"

"It was me that interdooced the gent to Stenger," growled the Double S foreman.

"I know the story," interrupted Sassoon. "What I want now is for you boys to fork your saddles and be on your way to the ranch. No need for you to hang around here." He drew Kile aside and the two men conversed in low tones.

"I git yuh," Banning heard the Double S foreman say.

The latter turned to him. "Come on, mister—let's git goin'."

"Reckon Sassoon's hit it plumb center," panted Banning's companion, as the two ran to overtake Brodie. "Betcha we ain't findin' that Injun layin' in that straw pile where I dumped him. He done that killin'—or I'm a sheepherder."

Brodie was waiting at the corral fence. "Where's that straw stack, Smoky?" he demanded. "Sure settles it if that Piute ain't there."

Kile led them around one of the big barns to the tumbled remains of a hay stack. There was no sign of the Indian. A search of the stables revealed that his pinto horse had likewise vanished.

"Sassoon had the right hunch," muttered Brodie. "The Piute done it—killed the doc." With a shrug he strode down the corral toward the house. Banning hurried after him.

"Hey—where yuh goin', mister?" called Smoky Kile. "Me an' you is ridin'—an' ridin' now."

"Left my hat in the house," Banning told him. "Ain't leavin' my Stetson behind, cowboy."

"Reckon I'll mosey along with yuh," said Smoky. He caught up with them—clutched Brodie's arm. "Say—Jim—what's the chance for a job at the Box B?"

The cattleman gave him a puzzled glance. "What's the big idea, Smoky? You've got a good job with the Double S outfit, ain't you? Or is Stenger handin' you your time?"

The Double S foreman spat in disgust. "Nothin' like that, Jim. Was figgerin' I ain't gettin' a fair deal with Nell. Kinda thought I had a chance with her till Clem Sanders come throwin' his loop. Now he's a wounded hero, she cain't even see me for his dust."

"That's your bad luck," snorted Nell's father. "You can bet your last peso I ain't handin' out no job to no cowboy to have him waste his time and my money, sparkin' my gal. Furthermore, and talkin' out loud, I don't aim to butt in on Nell's private and personal affairs."

The clatter of their feet on the patio stones brought Sanders hastily to the door. The girls were in the sitting room, he informed them.

"Left my hat in the doc's room," Banning told Smoky, turning down the corridor. Smoky hesitated, jealousy of Clem Sanders conflicting with his ill-concealed desire to keep the new Double S man under his eye. The sight of Clem following Brodie into the hall was too much for him. He hurried to overtake them. Banning's casual manner fell from him like a discarded cloak. Eager, alert, he darted into the little bedroom.

The body of Doc Spicer lay where it had fallen, almost directly under the window. Near the dead man was the chair on which Banning had tossed his black Stetson. He picked it up, pulled it over his dark hair, gaze fixed on the lifeless remains of Doc Spicer.

111

"Sure was fast work," he reflected. "One more second—and the King Buzzard would have been in Brodie's hands." He glanced cautiously at the open door and sank on one knee by the side of the dead man.

"Looks like a .45 made that hole," he muttered, "and when I searched that old Piute in the wine room, he had no gun on him. It wasn't the Indian who killed Doc Spicer." He got to his feet and went frowning from the little room.

A vague shape drifted toward him in the dark corridor. Banning halted, staring his surprise as Anita Callahan suddenly confronted him.

She looked at him silently for a moment, hand holding the folds of the rose-colored wrap tightly to her slim body, bare arms gleaming like old ivory against the dark background of night. He pulled off his battered Stetson, eyes mutely questioning her.

"Mr. Brodie tells me you are leaving us— immediately," she said, almost accusingly.

"It was Sassoon's orders," he explained. "Sorry to be ridin' off like this—" He shrugged. "What can I do? Sassoon's my boss—one of 'em."

"I don't want you to go," she surprisingly confessed. "I—I have found myself relying on you. I don't quite know why I feel this way about you—but I do—and I want you to stay."

"That's right kind of you, telling me that," stammered the cowboy. He shook his head. "Sure am sorry—but Sassoon wouldn't like me stayin' against his orders."

A little foot in a blue satin mule tapped the stone floor impatiently. "You can tell him you have changed your mind about working for the Double S," the girl said coolly. "You can tell him that you've decided to work for me—for the Cross Knife."

Banning hesitated, fingers twisting the brim of his hat. There was something he could not explain—his encounter with Smoky Kile and Stenger—in Lobo Pass—his very good reason for accepting Stenger's offer of a job with the Double S.

"Afraid I haven't much to say about it," he said miserably. "No, ma'am—reckon I've got to stick with the Double S—the way things are with me."

"I don't see why!" Surprise, indignation, crept into her voice. "You could be such a help at this time—what with Clem Sanders crippled—and the other boys—all dead. I'm sure Mr. Sassoon will be willing—"

"I can't explain," stammered Banning. "It's impossible. I have reasons—"

"Oh!" Anita eyed him doubtfully. "Well—I'm sorry you feel that way." Her tone grew scornful. "Perhaps you mean that you are—afraid?"

"That's not fair!" angrily protested the cowboy. "I'm trying to explain why I—I can't explain.

Maybe I can fix things later so I can quit the Double S."

Her former warm friendliness was gone. "Don't hurt yourself doing it on my account," she flung at him over her shoulder.

Instead of returning to the hall, she slipped through the door of her bedroom. Banning slowly pulled the Stetson back on his head. He seemed hurt, rather than angry. Smoky Kile's acid voice jerked his gaze down the corridor. The Double S foreman was striding toward him from the hall entrance.

"Come on, feller—let's ride." Smoky's voice was surly.

They fell into step, moving across the patio, the foreman muttering profanely under his breath. Banning saw that the man was seething with rage.

"What are you cussin' about, Smoky?" he queried innocently.

"Shut yore mouth," fumed Kile. "I'll fix that loud-talkin' Sanders," he added darkly. "I'll fix her, too."

They got their horses, Banning watering the stallion before they rode from the corral.

"Don't seem right—us riding away like this," he told the other man. He gestured at the silent, huddled forms against the corral fence. "These boys lying here—and Doc Spicer where he dropped."

"Sassoon an' Brodie will take care of 'em, come mornin'," replied Smoky indifferently. "Leave it to them. We've got plenty trouble of our own."

"I'll say we have," was Banning's unspoken comment. His thoughts went to that great herd of Cross Knife cattle now somewhere in Old Mexico—the cattle Stenger claimed to have rustled with the late Don Mike's connivance to evade seizure for debt by Asa Coons. It was in Banning's mind that the trouble pot had boiled fast and furious since he had ridden into Lobo Pass some nine or ten hours earlier that day.

They splashed through the shallows of Callahan's Crossing. Smoky Kile's slouching body straightened in the saddle.

"Ten more miles to go, cowboy," he said; "then the Double S—an' the good ol' hay—" His horse sprang forward under gouging spurs.

Gray gelding and bay stallion surged swiftly into the desert reaching blackly before them under a glittering sky. Gradually the splendor of the stars faded before a rising saffron tide in the east. . . .

The two men swung stiffly from their saddles. The weary horses stabled, Smoky led the way to the bunkhouse. In silence they shed gun belts and boots, careful not to disturb the snoring sleepers. Smoky Kile sighed sleepily and flung himself onto his bed.

"Blow out that light, will yuh, Banning?" he said drowsily.

Almost instantly his snores joined the crescendo. Eyeing him intently, Banning stealthily reached for the gun holster lying where Smoky had dropped it to the floor. He drew the six-shooter and closely scrutinized a moist stain discoloring the blue steel barrel.

Several hairs clung to the sticky smear of blood—dark, reddish hairs that had come from Banning's own head. With another cautious glance at the snoring Smoky, he carefully replaced gun and belt under the latter's cot and turned to blow out the lamp. From somewhere behind him came a stealthy hiss. Banning stiffened, startled gaze leaping round to the walrus-mustached face of old Windy Ben Allen grinning at him from a bunk near the door.

The young cowboy's narrowed gaze suddenly relaxed. On noiseless bare feet he went swiftly to the side of the old man and held out his hand for the piece of torn paper Ben had cautiously extracted from under his red flannel undershirt, a rough piece of wrapping paper, showing the crudely drawn outline of a broken ladder. Banning studied it for a moment, took a glance down the long room, and pulled a similar piece of paper from his shirt pocket. Roughly sketched on its brown surface was the outline of a frying pan. The broken edges of the two sheets of paper fitted exactly when Banning joined them. He gave Ben a glimmer of a smile. The latter nodded, winked, motioned for the young man to bend down.

"Figgered yuh was the man Brice was sendin'," he whispered in Banning's ear. "Sure glad yuh got here, son. There's a heap of work waitin' for yuh."

Chapter XI

Asa Coons looked wordlessly at the slim girl hesitating in his office doorway. The unwinking, yellow glare of those amber spectacles vaguely disturbed Anita. One never knew Asa Coons' thoughts by looking at him. He seemed so impenetrable, sitting behind those ever-present amber spectacles. She knew, of course, why he wore them, at least she had heard that a mine explosion had left him with a crippled leg and weakened eyes. . . . That was before he had settled in San Carlos and opened his private bank. Her grandfather had rather scoffed at Asa Coons and his bank. The Cross Knife always carried itself —there had never been need for Don Mike to borrow money.

The same was not true of other cattlemen in the Spanish Sinks. Asa Coons had prospered during the five years he had been in San Carlos. He was not popular—but he was respected and trusted. Even her grandfather had come to admit the man's integrity—and the violent Jim Brodie.

Asa Coons said in his startling bell-toned voice, "Why don't you come in, Miss Callahan? And please close the door. That sunshine—it hurts my eyes."

She gave him a timid, apologetic smile, closed the door quickly behind her.

"Makes me blind as a bat," Coons rumbled. "Couldn't make out who it was for a moment—standing there—staring at me. What made you stand there like that—watching me?"

"I thought you recognized me," said Anita, adding contritely, "I didn't realize the sunlight blinded you."

He gestured her to a chair near the desk. "I was expecting you," he told her. "You got my note, of course?"

"You said you had something important to tell me," admitted Anita. She gave him an eager look with eyes suddenly hard, feverishly bright. "I could suppose only one thing—that you have learned who killed grandfather—"

"Not that," said Coons slowly. "I'm sorry—if I raised your hopes."

The girl's slim body drooped visibly. "I couldn't think of anything else—important enough for you to send so urgent a message." Disappointment, indignation, edged her voice. "It is two weeks since it—it happened—and not a thing seems to have been done to track down the killers."

"The King Buzzard leaves no tracks," reminded Asa Coons.

Anita made a despairing gesture. "It's too horrible! This monster may be living right here in San Carlos. He may be any one of a score of ranchers in the Spanish Sinks. It's horrible to think of him and his killers laughing at us—at me!"

"We can only watch—and hope," Coons told her. "Some day he will go too far. When that day comes—he'll pay—with a rope around his neck."

"He's gone too far already," she said bitterly. "I'm going to do more than watch, Mr. Coons!"

The amber spectacles regarded her intently. "What do you mean, Miss Callahan?" Coons' long, bald head moved in warning dissent. "It is dangerous to openly defy the King Buzzard. You ought to know that—after what happened to Don Mike."

"Grandfather never even hinted to me that he had defied the King Buzzard," said the girl. "It was not his way to talk of his troubles to me." She looked tragically at the San Carlos banker. "It's all so mysterious! I don't understand why anyone should want to kill Don Mike! He was always so kind—so good!"

"Don Mike was a great gentleman," said Coons.

"How could they have done this thing to him?" she cried. "Oh, how could they?"

"He refused to obey the warning of the black feather," Asa Coons told her solemnly.

"The black feather? He did not tell me—"

"It was a warning for him to leave the Spanish Sinks—never to return," said Coons.

"How did you know Don Mike had been given the black feather?"

"He told me, my poor child." The deep voice was tenderly sympathetic—reluctant. "Don Mike was an honorable man. Because of a certain business matter between us he felt I should know his peril. I advised him to leave—for the time being—begged him not to worry about the money."

Anita gave him a wide-eyed, puzzled look. "The money!" she echoed. "What do you mean? I'm afraid I don't—don't understand."

"It is why I sent for you," explained the banker, his voice regretful. "I hated to add to your worries at this time, my child—but naturally you must know sooner or later about the matter." He paused. "Perhaps we might discuss it some other day—when you are feeling more fit for business."

"No," she told him in a faint voice. "Tell me now, Mr. Coons. Nothing can be as bad as the—the other thing that happened."

"I loaned Don Mike considerable money," went on the banker. His tone grew worried. "Didn't he speak of the matter to you, Miss Callahan?" She shook her head. "I took his note —and a chattel mortgage on the Cross Knife cattle," said Coons.

"How much?" There was a dazed, unbelieving expression in the girl's eyes.

"Quite a lot of money," he told her reluctantly. "Over two hundred thousand dollars, Miss Callahan."

"It—it doesn't seem possible," said Anita in a stunned voice. "Grandfather never borrowed.' When he needed money—he always sold cattle."

"He'd sold 'em down pretty close," Coons pointed out. "He couldn't afford to wreck his herd too much—what with the plans he had."

"But where has all that money gone?" she wanted to know. "I've had a statement from our bank in Cochise; our account there is less than a thousand." She paused, struck by a thought. "I forgot—he banked all this money with you, of course. I suppose you will have to take it back."

"It's not so simple as that," regretted the banker. "Unfortunately—Don Mike did not open an account with me." He shook his flat, bald head. "I'm afraid the money is all spent, my dear—gone into that desert land on the Big Anita. You know it was his dream to put the desert under irrigation."

"It was becoming more than a dream," she defended, resenting the sneer in his voice. "It was becoming a fact. The Cross Knife has over five thousand acres under water now—the best alfalfa land you ever saw."

"I'm afraid that does not help us much at this time," said Coons. "The fact remains that the Cross Knife owes me some two hundred thousand dollars—not counting interest, and the security—" The deep voice rolled at her with the merciless insistence of a storm-pushed sea—"the security has vanished."

"You mean—the cattle?" Anita looked at him, frightened, miserable, for the first time realizing the magnitude of the disaster.

"The cattle," echoed the banker solemnly. "Not much left on the Cross Knife since the raid, Miss Callahan."

"Very little," agreed Anita wearily. "Some yearlings—that were up in the Big Anita canyon—and most of the horses. Oh, what shall I do, Mr. Coons?" Her voice broke.

"I've been thinking it over," he told her. "Naturally—I can't afford to take such a heavy loss—"

Her dark head went up proudly. "It is not necessary to think I would allow you to lose the money."

The amber spectacles fixed her with a long silent stare. Anita found herself hysterically longing to snatch those masking lenses from the bony nose. It was like talking to a stone image, without expression, without emotion. He wasn't a living, breathing, human being—this Asa Coons; he was a piece of cold stone in man's dress, with a head carved long and flat and hairless, and yellow, staring eyes painted on the granite gray of the face, and a thin nose curved low to straight, chiseled lips. His sonorous, bell-toned voice was speaking again. She clung to it desperately. At least his voice was real—a living, rich melody of sound.

"It is hardly possible—probable, that you will want to keep the Cross Knife," he was saying; "it is too much responsibility for a girl—a young girl—"

"Give up the Cross Knife?" she exclaimed, aghast. "Why—Mr. Coons—how absurd! I am a Pinzon—as well as a Callahan! There has always been a Pinzon on the Cross Knife—ever since there was a Cross Knife."

"It does sound like sacrilege," admitted Asa Coons. "Perhaps you can suggest some other plan, Miss Callahan. Some way in which you can raise the money to repay me. You seemed indignant— when I mentioned that the loss was too big for me to bear."

"Suggest something else!" she stammered. Her troubled gaze went down to the tops of her shiny black boots. "I—I suppose I could borrow on the ranch. I really don't know much about such things." She looked at him, eyes resolute. "One thing you can be sure of—I'll never sell a foot of the Cross Knife. It is part of me—the last of the Pinzon-Callahans! Can't you understand how I feel, Mr. Coons? The thought of such a thing kills me!"

"It is unfortunate that you feel so deeply about

it," Coons told her with a worried shake of his bald head. "You can't afford to be sentimental—not if you wish to pay Don Mike's debt to me."

She stared at him with the dumb anguish of a trapped creature. He continued, shifting his gaze from the hurt, pleading eyes to a paper spread before him on the desk.

"You can't hope to borrow money on the ranch—the way things are; at least not enough to pay off Don Mike's note. The land is worthless—unless it is restocked. If you borrow money—you will need it for re-stocking the place. You can't do that—and pay me off."

"The land is not worthless!" she protested. "The irrigation—"

"As yet an experiment," he interrupted, "and one that has cost Don Mike a fortune. You say you have five thousand acres under water—alfalfa land—but where are your cattle? Be sensible, Miss Callahan."

"What is your plan?" Anita's voice was suddenly cool, her glance composed. "I suppose you mean —some arrangement about the ranch—something in the way of security?"

"That was in my mind," admitted Coons. "I can cancel the note—and give you fifty thousand dollars in cash—if you will give me a deed to the Cross Knife—a quit-claim deed. Such an arrangement takes a burden from your shoulders. You can go away—live comfortably wherever you choose." The banker shrugged. "It will be up to me to get my money back out of the ranch—if I can. I'm willing to try it—for the sake of Don Mike's granddaughter."

"I must think it over," she told him in a low voice. "Just now—it seems all beyond comprehension." She paused, smooth brow puckered. "You have the paper, Mr. Coons? The thing grandfather signed about the cattle?"

"Of course." Coons picked up the paper from the desk and held it out. She took it gingerly, her expression bewildered as she glanced at the closely-penned lines. The legal phraseology was too much for her, she confessed.

"I suppose it is all just as you say—even if I don't understand it," she said.

"He put his name to it," Coons pointed out. "You know Don Mike's handwriting, don't you?"

She nodded, eyes absorbed with the virile scrawl at the bottom of the sheet. "Yes, Mr. Coons. I know Don Mike's signature." She gave the banker a puzzled glance.

"What is it?" He spoke sharply, hand reaching for the paper. "You seem surprised. Do you deny that is Don Mike's signature?"

"Why—no, Mr. Coons. I—I suppose it was a shock—seeing his name on a chattel mortgage," explained Anita, vaguely uneasy under his blind, glassy stare. She stood up. "I'll think the matter over—about your offer."

The banker nodded. "It is the only solution," he insisted.

"Jim Brodie thinks some effort should be made to track the cattle thieves. He says that even Mexico can't swallow up a herd of over four thousand white-faced cattle without leaving some clew."

"Jim Brodie is a loud-talking fool," grumbled Asa Coons. He snorted angrily. "Does he expect the United States to start a war over your Cross Knife steers?"

"Jim Brodie is a fine man," she defended. "If he knew where my cattle were—in Mexico—or any other place, he wouldn't wait for the United States army to get them back for me."

"I don't question it. I'd do as much myself," Coons assured her. He reached for his crutches and lifted himself from the chair. "Brodie will get into trouble," he warned. "He'll get the black feather—if his talk reaches the King Buzzard."

The girl paled. Coons leaned on his crutches, useless leg dangling, long, hairless head sunk forward, a shaft of sunlight striking yellow fire from his amber spectacles. Anita shivered. There was something formidable about Asa Coons as he hung there on his crutches, something oddly repellent—frightening.

"See," he said in his booming voice. He pointed a crutch at the door. "The King Buzzard left that for me—the night Don Mike lay dead at the Cross Knife."

"The *black feather!*" she whispered, staring fearfully at the long-bladed knife thrust in the wall over the door. Bound to the haft was a small black feather.

"He left one for Sassoon," Coons told her grimly. "You can see it—if you care to look. Stuck in the sign of the Horsehead." For the first time Coons showed emotion, the dark, gray skin of his face wrinkling in a mirthless smile. "Sassoon swears he will leave it there till he can put it in the King Buzzard's heart."

"I can't stand any more!" gasped the girl. "I don't see how you can laugh! Oh, it is too horrible—" She fled to the door—jerked it open. "I can't help it," she told him a bit hysterically. "I'm afraid I haven't got hold of myself—yet. Please forgive me, Mr. Coons. And I'll think it over—about the ranch." The door closed behind her slim, black figure.

Asa Coons stood for a minute, wide-shouldered body hunched forward on the crutches, gaze fixed on the door. Again came the mirthless smile, wrinkling gray, leathery skin. Lifting a big hand he removed the amber spectacles and polished the lenses against the sleeve of his loose, black alpaca coat, small, shiny, gun-metal eyes fixed reflectively on the sinister knife in the wall. They were curiously opaque eyes, expressionless, unwinking—and sunk deep under bony brows.

Chapter XII

Anita rode slowly down the street, past the Horsehead Bar, past Asa Coons' office, turning at the corner into a road that was little more than a rough trail, bending down to the tule flats of Frio Creek. Engrossed with her dismal thoughts, she did not see Joe Sassoon, standing just inside the low swing doors of the saloon. As she swung from the street, he emerged from the dim interior and spoke to an old Indian dozing under the shade of the awning.

"Chico—you see white squaw go down street?" Sassoon jerked thumb at the flurry of dust lifting above the corner building. "White squaw maybe go Old Town. You catchum trail quick and tell me what she do in Old Town."

"*Si*," grunted the Indian. "Chico catchum squaw." He rose stiffly, selected a hammer-headed pinto from among the horses tied in front of the saloon and rode away at a jog trot.

A group of riders tore into the street, trailing a banner of yellow dust. The Double S outfit, Sassoon saw, with Al Stenger leading the procession. It was payday, and outfits from the ranches were already whooping it up in the Horsehead, and across the street at Dutch Jake's place. Sassoon knew that before morning most of those paychecks would be in his own strong safe. Even the money of those who favored Dutch Jake's place eventually came to his pockets. Only Dutch Jake knew that Joe Sassoon was the actual owner of the Palace Bar.

Sassoon's eyes suddenly narrowed. Well to the front of the approaching riders was a tall man on a great bay stallion. The new hand, Cal Banning. He had not seen Banning since that night at the Cross Knife hacienda. The man had not impressed him too favorably. A fugitive from the law—a killer—lightning fast with his guns. There were others like him on the Double S payroll—but this Cal Banning was of different caliber. He could think as fast and true as he could work his six-guns. He was too intelligent for Al Stenger's mental equipment to cope with, and that made him dangerous. He could make a fool of Stenger. The saloon man's eyes glittered. He turned quickly into the long barroom.

"Tell Stenger I want to see him soon as he gets in," he told the bartender. "And Monte—tell him I said for him to lay off the liquor."

It was all of thirty minutes before Sassoon's redheaded partner pushed through the office door and lowered his bulk into a chair by the desk.

"What's on yore mind, Joe?" The cattleman's tone was sulky. "Monte says yuh want to palaver."

Sassoon gave him a sour look. "Didn't Monte give you my message?"

"Sure he did," grumbled Stenger. "Where yuh git that way, Joe? I ain't yore dog, to be runnin' at yore call." As usual when he had a few drinks in him, Stenger was sullenly belligerent. "Ain't likin' yuh regulatin' my likker," he told Sassoon.

"You're my partner," reminded the latter coldly. "A damned useless partner—when you're full of whiskey. You've got to watch your step. There's a storm movin' over this way, feller. That's why I want you to go light on the drinks."

"Huh?" Stenger blinked small, red eyes. "Whatcha mean—storm—?"

Sassoon curved a thumb at the noisy barroom. "Why isn't Cal Banning out there with the rest of the boys?"

"Cal?" Stenger grinned. "Say, Joe—you'll laugh when I tell yuh—"

"I'm asking you—where is Cal Banning? Thought he rode into town with you."

"I'm tellin' yuh about him," growled the cattleman. "Reckon Cal is down in Old Town by now. Figgered he'd git him that pair of silver spurs he'd heard old Cordero has hangin' in his cantina. One of the boys—Slim, it was—tells him about them old Pinzon bronc ticklers, and Cal swears he's buyin' them if it takes all the cash he's got—includin' two weeks' pay I give him."

"Old Town!" Sassoon's voice was brittle with anger. "You fool! Didn't I send you word by Smoky Rile never to let him go anywhere alone—"

"Dontcha git oneasy, Joe," reassured his partner. "I got Slim trailin' him. There ain't nothin' he does but what me an' you knows pronto." He grinned across the desk at the perturbed Sassoon. "Was tellin' yuh how yuh'd laugh about him an' old Windy Ben Allen. Fust thing he does was to jump that there old coot yuh framed me to take on as cook. Said Ben's cakes was hawgfood. Joke was—old Ben never cooked them cakes. Knowed you wasn't really wantin' me to fire Tubby Jones—an' them flapjacks was Tubby's own breakfast top-notchers as per usual. But Cal—he goes an' jumps Ben an' tells me if Ben's cook we're losin' a top-hand name of Cal Banning. Old Windy gits sore—drags out that cannon of his an' goes on the warpath. Likewise Tubby for reasons personal—goes huntin' for his own six-shooter. Took all of us to keep Ben an' Tubby from committin' suicide." Stenger's round, red head wagged solemnly. "Them two would have had no chance a-tall agin them black-handled guns Cal wears.

"Funny thing about it," continued the cattleman, scowling, "this here Windy Ben does a fadeaway on us. Sulks in the bunkhouse all day, an' come mornin'—he's gone—an' one of our best broncs with him."

"You blundering fool!" snarled Sassoon. "Didn't I warn you to keep an eye on him?"

"The old coot can't do us no harm," protested

Stenger. "No sense worryin' about him, Joe."

"I warned you," fumed Sassoon. "I told you Ben Allen's talk against Jim Brodie was a foxy play to win our confidence. Why didn't you send me word that he'd skipped?"

"Yuh're all wet," argued Stenger. "Yuh should have heard the names he called Jim Brodie the night we rode out to the Double S. Only thing that has me sore is him takin' that horse."

"Al," said Sassoon, "Ben Allen was a plant. Don't fool yourself."

"Yuh mean it?" Stenger's voice was suddenly apprehensive. "Yuh mean somebody is cuttin' sign on us?" He glared across the desk. "What would Windy Ben pull his freight for so quick—if he was planted to spy on us?"

"Because your new man—Cal Banning—told him to go. They framed that quarrel to fool you. Most likely that old rannihan is nosin'. the ground for more sign right now—under Banning's orders."

"You're talkin' over my haid," grumbled Stenger. "Don't git yuh a-tall. What's Cal Banning got to do with old Ben? Cal is on the run from the law—a hunted killer. He's got every reason to play his hand with us."

"He's phony," insisted the saloon man. "I studied him that night at the Cross Knife. He don't carry the earmarks of a hunted outlaw."

Stenger lurched from his chair. "I'll take him

133

apart!" he said furiously. "Fool Al Stenger, huh? I'll show the double-crossin' sidewinder—" He turned to the door.

"Sit down!" rasped Sassoon. "We've got to get him right. He's smart—too smart for you."

Stenger resumed his chair, fingers closing around the whiskey bottle the gambler pushed toward him. "Well—what's yore idee? Whatcha goin' to do with him?"

"Leave him to me," answered the other man softly. "All you've got to do is watch your step with him. He mustn't guess that we suspect him." Sassoon paused, frowned. "Queer about Doc Spicer's Indian," he added. "Smoky any idea what happened to him?"

"Guess you know as much as I do about that Injun," returned the cattleman. He gave Sassoon a wicked wink. "If that old Piute is where Doc Spicer is—he's sure one good Injun by now."

"That's just what we don't know," worried Sassoon. "If he is as dead as Doc Spicer—I'd like to know it. That's where the shoe's pinching. That old Piute thought a lot of the doc. He'll likely make trouble."

"What did happen to the doc?" queried Stenger. "I mean—who did bump him off?"

"Use your noodle," sneered Sassoon. "Who else but the King Buzzard—you dumb fool?" He rapped out an oath. "Happened just at the wrong time. Jim Brodie would have liked to pin it on me—or Smoky—only he knew he couldn't make it stick."

"Smoky said Spicer was about to spill all he knew about the King Buzzard when he was shot." Stenger leered at his companion. "Tough luck—him gettin' that bullet in his spine. Sure would have busted up the Buzzard gang if he'd told what he knew to Brodie, huh, Joe?"

"It's playing tag with dynamite—fooling with the King Buzzard," Sassoon told him grimly. "Brodie will likely find that out if he doesn't lay off. Why didn't Smoky Kile come in with you boys?" he added in an irate voice. "Wanted to talk to him about that Piute. It's up to Smoky to get on that Indian's trail."

"Smoky's gone courtin' him a gal," grinned the Double S boss. "All dolled up like a range Romeo."

"Brodie's girl?" Sassoon frowned. "The fool! He's not welcome over at the Box B. It'll mean gunplay if Clem Sanders runs into him."

"That'll be Clem's bad luck," Stenger assured him. The cattleman scowled. "Only one jasper I know of can beat Smoky to the draw—Cal Banning." Stenger added a lurid oath.

There was an ugly glint in the saloon man's black eyes. He leaned across the desk. "Listen," he said softly; "Banning won't worry you—or anyone else—after tonight. I've a plan to trip him up—"

Chapter XIII

Cal Banning reined his bay stallion under the giant umbrella trees densely shading the weather-beaten adobe walls of Cordero's cantina. The long front of the ancient hostelry rose two storeys, with an upper balcony of iron grill-work screening tall, narrow windows that looked upon the crumbling ruins of a church across the tiny plaza.

Among the several horses tied in front of the cantina was an animal that Banning recognized. Anita Callahan's speedy chestnut mare. Wondering what business could have brought the girl down to the Mexican quarter in Old Town, he made the stallion fast to a staple driven into one of the trees and turned for a look at the cantina's doorway.

Soft Spanish voices came to him, mingled with the twanging of a guitar—an old tune that Banning knew and liked—La Paloma. He hummed the refrain, smiling a friendly greeting as two Mexicans appeared in the entrance, swarthy faces shaded under enormous, high-peaked sombreros.

"*Buenas dias*, *amigos*," he said. "Is this the cantina of Gaspar Cordero?"

"*Si*," answered one of the men, after a moment's startled scrutiny. He muttered to his companion, and both hastily withdrew into the dim interior. There was a sudden hush, followed by the shuffle of slippered feet. A third man appeared in the low doorway, a guitar dangling from one hand.

"You wish to see me, Señor? I am Gaspar Cordero."

"*Si*, Señor." Banning smiled. "I am told that you have a pair of silver spurs. It is my wish to see them—perhaps buy them."

The man stared at him with inscrutable eyes. For all his lack of height he was an impressive figure—enormously wide across the shoulders, herculean-limbed, broad, dark face indicating a strong Indian strain. Coarse white hair rose like a lion's mane from massive head, and sunken brown eyes looked piercingly from under bristling black brows. His nose was high, with flaring nostrils— a ragged white mustache covered wide, thin-lipped mouth. His age was indeterminate—as if the years had ceased to take toll, leaving him hard, durable—like a toughened piece of seasoned brown oak. A curiously intent, startled expression crept into the bright, sunken eyes as he spoke.

"You are—from where, Señor?"

"Banning's my name. Ridin' for the Double S outfit."

An odd disappointment flickered across the innkeeper's impassive face. He shook his head. Double S men were not welcome at his cantina, he bluntly told Banning. As for the silver spurs—

they were not for sale. With a shrug he turned away.

"One moment, Señor," called Banning softly. "What if I should tell you that I am a friend of the Señorita Callahan?"

Cordero's great bulk grew suddenly rigid, massive head turning slowly in a backward stare at the tall cowboy.

"She is here—is it not so?" continued the cowboy, gesturing at the chestnut mare. "It is important that I see her, Señor Cordero."

For a moment the inscrutable eyes probed him with merciless intentness. Banning fidgeted, sensing growing menace, suspicion, in the man's manner.

"If you will tell her," he suggested.

"And your friend—he wishes to see the señorita—too?" Cordero's voice was threatening. He made an angry gesture with the guitar.

"Friend?" echoed Banning, surprised. He broke off, stared in the direction indicated by the pointing guitar. A rider was dismounting under the umbrella trees—Slim Dotton—a Double S man. Banning's eyes went hard.

"Listen," he muttered to the inn-keeper. "That man has been sent to spy on me. If you are a friend of Miss Callahan—get him out of the way."

Cordero hesitated, flung the approaching Double S man an uneasy glance. "How do I know that you are a friend of the señorita's?" he demanded. "Quick—Señor—convince me!"

"I'll convince you," Banning told him coolly. He pushed swiftly past the old man into the dim interior of the cantina, vaguely conscious of startled, staring eyes watching him as he drew Cordero close. "The spurs—quick—show them to me. I will give you proof that you can trust me as a friend."

Cordero gave him a sharp look—went quickly behind the bar, Banning watching in a fever of impatience. Outside he could hear the crunching of Slim Dotton's boots nearing the door. Cordero was bending down to a shelf. His wide, powerful shoulders lifted.

"The spurs, Señor," he said in a low voice. He placed them reverently on the shining black surface of the bar. Banning eyed them, his face oddly pale. He seemed dazed, overcome by some inexplicable emotion—as when he had looked at the little miniature of the first Don Mike Callahan.

"The proof, Señor," reminded Cordero, watching him closely.

Slim Dotton paused in the low entrance, grinning gaze impudently meeting unfriendly stares.

Banning darted him a swift glance and took up the spurs, of Mexican make, with huge rowels and heavily embossed with silver. "You will have the proof," he muttered. With thumb and forefinger he pressed the silver button fastening the strap of richly-carved Spanish leather to the solid silver heel clamp. The button slid from a groove. He turned it over. Inside the little locket-like face was a tiny miniature of a baby boy—a baby with bluish-gray eyes and dark red hair.

There was a low, astonished exclamation from the intent inn-keeper. "The baby picture of Don Mike," he muttered, "the señorita's grandfather!" He stared at Banning, excitement gleaming in the sunken eyes.

The latter nodded, snapped the silver button back into place and seized the other spur. "And this, my friend, is the twin brother—said by some to have died in infancy." He thumbed off the silver button, turning it over in his palm. The tiny, thumb-nail miniature it contained was a replica of the first—with the exception of the hair, which was darker.

"Satisfied?" queried Banning softly. "Proof enough, my friend?"

"*Si*," muttered Cordero. He seemed shaken to the roots of his being. "I thought only I knew the secret of these spurs, Señor. How is it that you—also know?"

Banning looked at him searchingly. "Can you guess—Gaspar Cordero?"

"*Si—si*—I am sure—" The old man's voice was shaky—exultant. "But it is beyond belief!"

"You were a young vaquero when Anita Pinzon painted these pictures of her babies," said

Banning. "She had them placed in these spurs—a gift for the faithful one she had chosen to always guard her Don Mike's sons."

"I put the little Don Mike on his first horse," muttered Cordero with the reminiscent pride of many years. "I teach him to ride—" His seamed, walnut face was suddenly grief-stricken; "but the other little son—ah—Dios forgive me!"

"It was not your fault," said Banning gently. He glanced over his shoulder. Slim Dotton was sauntering to the bar. The man grinned.

"How yuh makin' out with the bronc-ticklers, Cal?" he wanted to know. "If yuh make a deal, I claim yuh owe me a round of drinks, cowboy."

"No deal, Slim," Banning told him in a disappointed voice. "But I'm buyin' anyhow." He looked at Cordero who silently reached down a bottle of wine and slid it along the bar with a fierce glance at the grinning Double S man.

"I not like your Double S frien's," he muttered to Banning sullenly. He looked at the big silver spurs for a moment. "I teach him to ride," he repeated—"and now—" He glanced at the young man, sunken brown eyes gleaming pools of hate. "And now he lies in his grave—slain—the little Señorita's gran'father—slain!" Slowly he returned the spurs to their hiding-place under the bar. "I will take you to her—" His lips barely moved. "But first—I will fix him." In a louder voice, audible to all in the cantina, he said, "It is so,

141

Señor—I cannot sell my spurs to you. They are not for sale. But to prove my good will, I will open a bottle of my best wine for the señor—and his frien'." Smiling affably, the inn-keeper shuffled down the length of the bar and disappeared through a narrow door.

"These wine ver' old," he told them, reappearing with a dusty bottle. "I keep him lock in safe place."

He drew the cork with a resounding *plop* that brought a pleased, expectant grin to Slim Dotton's hard mouth.

"Ver' old wine," Cordero repeated softly, filling the three glasses he set before them. "But one leetle moment, Señor," he apologized, "these cork in your glass! I will remove it." He took Slim's glass and bent low behind the bar, seizing a spoon from the shelf behind him. "There—it is gone," he smiled, replacing the glass in front of the Double S man. "Drink 'earty—as you gringo vaqueros say it." He lifted his glass—they drank.

"Some vino," sighed Slim. He put his glass down and leaned against the bar.

"The señor like the wine?" queried the inn-keeper softly, eyes intent on the man. He refilled the glass from the dusty bottle, his other hand brushing over the rim, apparently at a fly.

"*Gracias.*" Slim grinned foolishly at his host and noisily emptied the second glass. "Some vino," he repeated in a sleepy voice. He leaned heavily against the bar—turned reproachful gaze on Banning. "Whash matter—ol' timer? Why ain't yuh drinkin' glash for glash—yuh ol' maverick?"

"Plenty of time," Banning rejoined. "Don't wait for me, Slim." He exchanged glances with the inn-keeper. The latter smiled grimly—refilled the cowboy's glass.

"Ain't one to drink alone," grumbled Slim. He blinked around at dark faces silently watching from the surrounding dimness. "Step up, hombres —it's bottles out—an' name yore own pizen," he invited. "My treat—gents." He flung a gold coin on the bar.

There was a moment's silence, then a scraping of feet as Cordero began setting out bottles. Some half dozen Mexicans lined up on either side of the Double S cowboy, teeth showing white in sinister, derisive smiles. The inn-keeper shuffled from behind the bar and picked up his guitar.

"We will sit here, Señor," he said to Banning, pulling out a chair. His great fingers moved idly over the strings, picking out lazy chords that resolved into the plaintive strains of La Paloma.

Banning wanted to laugh. There was something inexpressibly incongruous, absurd, the way those huge, gnarled fingers tenderly caressed the strings—bringing out the melody of the dainty little love song.

"Soon—he will be *muy* shut-eye—sleeping,"

muttered the guitar-player. "You saw, Señor? What I do weeth his glass?"

Banning nodded. Cordero's smile was scornful. "He will never suspec'. He only theenk he drink too much strong vino." Cordero strummed another lazy chord. "I have always play the guitar. When I was yong—I play at wedding of the Señorita Anita Pinzon when she marry the first Don Mike—he who was our leetle señorita's great gran-father."

"That makes you out an old man," observed Banning. He stared curiously at the rugged bulk overflowing the chair.

"I was a young man—when our Don Mike was born," said Cordero simply. He shrugged massive shoulders, struck another chord. "Old—*si*—but not too old to forget—not too old to help the leetle señorita, Señor." He broke off. "Ah—your gringo frien'—these spy—he no feel so good!"

Slim Dotton was staggering toward them, a glass in unsteady hand, the wine splashing crimson splotches on the hard, earthen floor.

"Sure feelin' queer," he mumbled in a drowsy voice as he lurched up. He stood, swaying on his feet and lifted the glass to his lips. It slipped from his fingers—tinkled on the floor. Slim giggled foolishly. "Some vino—yuh tellum, fellers." Knees sagged under him and he collapsed into Banning's reaching arms.

"In these room, Señor." Cordero grinned

malevolently at the senseless cowboy as Banning carried him through the door the inn-keeper opened.

They went a short distance down a dark, narrow hall to a small room where Banning dumped the already snoring man on a pile of sacks in the corner.

"He will sleep for long time," commented Cordero in a satisfied voice. He looked at Banning. "Now, Señor—I will take you to the señorita."

He led the way down the corridor and up a stairway to an upper hall. Banning spoke in a warning voice.

"Don't tell her anything, Cordero. About the silver spurs, I mean."

The old man gave him an astonished look. "Not tell her, Señor?"

"No—not a word," insisted the young man. "I want her to take me on trust—without knowing what you know, Cordero."

"As you will," agreed the inn-keeper dubiously. His piercing eyes searched the other man. "You have met the señorita—no?"

"At the Cross Knife," admitted Banning. "The night Doc Spicer was killed. I went there with Sassoon—to be with the body of Don Mike."

"She—she does not suspec'?"

"No."

Still the old man hesitated. "You speak of Doc

Spicer. That is strange, Señor. It is because of him that she is here—*one* reason why she is in this room upstairs—now." He darted the young man a triumphant look. "You will onderstan'—when I open these door." He pushed the door open, motioning Banning inside.

The latter took one quick glance and swung on heel, hand darting to gun, anger, suspicion, in his eyes. "What's the game, Cordero? The room's empty—there's no girl in here!"

The inn-keeper's astonishment was too sincere to question. He stared blankly around. "But she—she was here—the señorita was here," he stammered. "I left her here a few moments before you came to the cantina, Señor." He gestured at what Banning had taken for a bundle of bedding in a corner of the room. "And the room—it is not empty—as you can see—"

Banning stared at the bundle of bedding. As Cordero claimed—the room was not empty. A man lay under those blankets—a still, silent form, scarcely discernible in the gloom.

Banning gave the inn-keeper a puzzled, wondering look. "Who is he—that you should bring Miss Callahan to see him?"

"That man, Señor—is Piute Pete," Gaspar Cordero said very softly. "Doc Spicer's servant, Señor."

"The Piute?"

Banning's eyes gleamed with quick excitement.

"The missing Indian, huh?" he muttered. He went noiselessly to the pile of bedding and stooped for a closer scrutiny of the dark, leathery face. The man was breathing, he observed, and not dead, as he appeared to be.

"How did he get here?" he asked Cordero.

The latter shrugged. "No one knows—but himself—and the man who knifed him." Cordero shook his head. "Three knife wounds in the back! A tough hombre—these Piute. Dios knows how he live to come all the way from the Cross Knife. He breathes—but that is all."

"He must not die," said Banning fiercely. "Cordero—he's got to live—live long enough to talk." He eyed the old man queerly. "Why should he have come to you, Cordero?"

"He is an Indian—and an Indian wants revenge," answered Cordero. His smile was grim. "Perhaps he knew one man—who might help him get that revenge, Señor. You—who know the secret of the silver spurs—should onderstan' what I mean."

"I think I do, Gaspar Cordero."

Banning's voice was affectionate and he added a phrase in soft Spanish that meant "old and faithful friend," at which the aged man's deep eyes went inexpressibly tender. It was a phrase that he knew well—one worked in delicate silver letters around the clasp of one of the spurs given him by the great-grandmother of

Anita Callahan. The clasp of the companion spur bore his name in similar silver lettering.

"But the señorita," he worried. "I left her in these room. She is not now in these room. She wished to see these man—we think maybe he talk—tell us what happen that night at the rancho."

"How did she know he was here?" demanded Banning curiously.

"She no know. She come to see me about another business—" Cordero hesitated. "Men are afraid of the Cross Knife. They fear these King Buzzard—will not work for her. She think maybe I find her some vaqueros—good men to trust—who no be afraid of death." He nodded grimly. "I have two such hombres—good vaqueros—who fear not the evil one himself. You saw them, Señor—as you rode into my yard."

Banning nodded, recalling the two swarthy men. Lean, hard-fighting men, he had sized them up.

"She wanted me," he told Cordero. "I couldn't —then. There were reasons hard to explain—dangerous reasons." He frowned. "Still the same reasons why I shouldn't—but man—it's hell—must be hell for her—worse than she knows!" Banning broke off—hurled himself at the window that opened on the iron balcony.

Chapter XIV

It was no mere impulse that took Anita to Old Town to see Gaspar Cordero. She had, for days, contemplated something of the kind, hesitating only because she feared drawing sinister attention to one she had long regarded as quite incapable of further interest in the things of life.

The stories of Gaspar Cordero were legend, she recalled. During the latter years of the first Don Mike's time, he had been majordomo of the Cross Knife hacienda—a man of might—of daring deeds. It was the interview with Asa Coons —the devastating discovery that the fate of the Cross Knife hung in the balance—that resolved out of her muddled conjecturings the fixed determination to seek out Gaspar Cordero.

He was an amazement to her. She had not seen him in years, since childhood days. She found him incredible—but a living actuality of reassurance and comfort. Overcome, she wept as she had not wept the day she found Don Mike lying stark in his own doorway. Her dark head against Gaspar's massive chest, she let the tears flow, he holding her close in powerful arms as once he had held her long years before when the death of a pet dog had brought her in tears to him for comfort.

"I am glad that you have come at last, Señorita," he told her in Spanish. "If you had not come to me soon—I would have gone to you. I am not the horseman I was," he added grimly. "The years have piled on me like the gray rocks on El Toro."

"You are magnificent," she told him, using the mother tongue of the Pinzons. "As old as El Toro—yes—but as strong as El Toro." She looked at him with kindling eyes. "Just to see you—be with you—makes me strong again. There—I'm done with shedding tears. I'm a Callahan," she reminded him. "Callahans have always been fighters, Gaspar Cordero."

"That is good talk," he applauded. "And now, Señorita, let me know all that you know. It is not much that I have heard—but enough to know that evil minds conspire against the Cross Knife. There is purpose in the methods of the one we call the King Buzzard."

"A purpose?" Anita's voice was puzzled. "You think that these—these killings are related—that they are merely a means to some specific end— some man's ambition?"

"Things come to my ears," said Gaspar Cordero; "little things that bit by bit I weave into a tale that some day will startle the Spanish Sinks. Perhaps the time is near when my tale may be told." He paused, shook his head. "But not yet. Cunning must be met with cunning." He looked at her. "Don Mike was here—the day before he was slain. And he was afraid. Tell me all that you know, Señorita."

She told him the story as she knew it—from the time of finding the dead longhorn—the fatal premonition of the black feather fluttering from the sky to settle on the horns of the giant Cross Knife steer.

Cordero gave her a strange look when she came to the interview with Asa Coons. It was unlike Don Mike, was his puzzled comment. Don Mike had made no mention of such a transaction—yet it must be so, for the señorita had seen the paper with her own eyes.

"Don Mike intimated that he feared for his life—that he had received the warning of the black feather—that if the worst came to the worst—he depended on me to help you," Cordero told her. "He did not speak of this cattle loan—which is strange—strange."

Anita eyed the old man thoughtfully. There was something about the paper Asa Coons had shown her that troubled her. She would, she decided, tell Gaspar of the circumstances. His voice broke into her hurried reflections.

"The Piute, suspected of killing Doc Spicer—is here," he informed her.

She stared at him, thunderstruck.

"Doc Spicer's Indian! Here—in this house?"

"He came the next day," said Cordero. "It does not seem possible he can still be alive—unless it

151

be a Divine Providence that he live to tell us what he must know."

"You mean he is—hurt?"

"Stabbed in the back—practically a dead man. He has not yet spoken a word."

Anita rose from her chair. "Where is he? I must see him," she told Cordero.

"You cannot hope he is ready to talk, yet," he warned. "But follow me, Señorita. He is hidden in an upper room."

She followed him upstairs, to stare dumbly at the limp form lying in the blankets.

"I feel faint," she said in a choked voice. "It—it brings that dreadful night back to me."

"Come away," advised Cordero. "There is nothing to be done—now."

She shook her head, fascinated gaze on the unconscious Indian. "No—I think someone should be with him constantly. See—he seems to stir! No, Gaspar—let me stay for a while. He may—may find strength to speak."

"I will get you a glass of water—or no—a little wine," decided Cordero, eyeing her keenly. "For a little while then, you can stay, Señorita." He went out on soundless feet.

Anita went to the tall, narrow window, wondering if she dare open it. The room was close—she felt the need of fresh air.

Directly below was the little plaza, with the ruins of the ancient church across the way.

152

Beyond the great umbrella trees she could see the crumbling tower where still hung the bells brought from old Spain by a long-gone Pinzon. Her glance roved down to the shaded yard in front of the cantina. A tall man was riding in on a big bay horse. Anita knew that satiny-coated, blood-bay stallion—and she knew the lean hawk face under that worn black Stetson. Startled, she drew back from the window.

What was Cal Banning doing in Old Town—at Cordero's cantina? She ventured another look, apprehension deepening in her dark eyes as she saw a second rider turning into the plaza. She had seen that man before. He was one of Al Stenger's hard-faced Double S men. That was Cal Banning's outfit, she recalled with some bitterness; the outfit he had refused to quit for her own employ—despite her need—her almost self-abasement before him. He had said that there were reasons why he could not leave the Double S—reasons he could not explain.

Anita's lovely mouth curved in a scornful smile. No doubt there were reasons—shameful reasons. She had heard rumors regarding the Double S riders—rumors that said most of them were hunted outlaws—gunmen—killers—a bad lot. And Cal Banning chose to throw in his lot with such riff-raff—rather than accept decent employment with the Cross Knife. Dangerous employment—yes—but honest. Like the rest of them—he was riff-raff—a coward—a plain no-good. She was lucky, Anita told herself, that her attempt to hire him had failed. He might have been capable of any treachery to her.

Another thought worried her. What did it portend—this presence of Double S men at Cordero's cantina? It was unusual for gringo cowboys to patronize Cordero's. They did not associate with the Mexican vaqueros when it came to their drinking—their carousings. It looked suspicious, Anita frantically told herself. There was something up—some hidden menace. She reproached herself for coming to Cordero—involving him—perhaps dangerously—in her precarious affairs. He was too old to combat dangers. She stole another glance out of the window, saw Banning pause in front of the cantina door. He was handsome, Anita decided. She could not deny that he was a splendid-looking man. It seemed incredible that he was—well—a bad lot—perhaps an enemy. For the first time she realized the sinister circumstances of her first meeting with Cal Banning. The freshly-trampled cattle trail leading into Lobo Pass—the dead longhorn—Banning and Al Stenger encountering her as they rode out of the pass—Stenger's statement that it was queer they had seen nothing of the cattle. How could they have failed to see—or meet a herd so recently headed into the pass?

Anita's golden brown eyes turned black with

anger, resentment. She had been blind. The longhorn's death had been no mystery to Stenger and Banning! How they must have laughed at her innocent acceptance of their story! Frowningly she struggled to recall other incidents of that encounter at the side of the dead longhorn steer. Yes—she remembered now—Banning's queer expression when Al Stenger talked about the cattle. He knew all the time that Stenger and he had seen the cattle—must have—must have been with the murderers of Don Mike—were actually the leaders of the gang that had raided the Cross Knife!

Her brain was in a whirl. She was going quite mad, she told herself wildly. It couldn't be—it just couldn't. She had no right—accusing Al Stenger of being the King Buzzard. He was a neighbor—an unpleasant neighbor, perhaps—and his men a rough, hard lot—but that was no reason for her to jump to ugly conclusions. Plenty of cattlemen were rough and tough men—and cowboys were never considered exactly saintly. She thought of Sassoon. Sassoon was Stenger's partner. Sassoon was cultured—really a fine gentleman. It would be impossible for Stenger to be the King Buzzard —that ruthless killer—and Sassoon unaware of it. Anita smiled ruefully. Why—she was being absurd—allowing her nerves to lead her into a veritable maze of insane conjectures. Sassoon was a reassuring thought. Sassoon was the last man in the world to suspect—and he was Al Stenger's partner in the Double S.

Her mind went back to Banning. Whatever he was—or wanted at Cordero's—he must not find her here. She did not care to see him—she couldn't stand seeing him, she said to herself, she just couldn't!

She went back to the wounded Indian, examining him more closely this time. She saw that he had really been skillfully bandaged—that all that could be accomplished for him had been done. There was actually nothing she could do to hasten the man's recovery. It was senseless—waiting to hear his story. She could leave all that to Gaspar Cordero. She moved on quick, noise-less feet to the door. Her mind was made up—she would find some way out of the cantina—some back door—get her mare and escape from the place before chance brought her face to face with Cal Banning.

The narrow stairs, she found, afforded the only descent to the lower hall. Silently she crept down and reached the dim corridor. She paused, listened. Men's voices came faintly from the main room. She could hear the clink of glasses, and presently, the lazy twanging of a guitar. The tune was La Paloma.

Anita remembered now that Gaspar Cordero had been famous for his skill with the guitar—that La Paloma was his favorite tune.

The music suddenly hushed—she heard a drunken, complaining voice—the unmistakable sound of glass breaking on the earthen floor. Suddenly panic-stricken, she fled down the dim corridor, turning through the first door she saw.

It was a bedroom—the windows heavily shaded—and inset with iron bars, giving it a cell-like effect. Anita sensed she was in Gaspar Cordero's private room. Ancient vaquero trappings festooned the walls; queer, high-decked saddles, savage-bitted bridles, spurs, reatas—a pair of wide-spreading horns. It was here that the old man kept the memories of a long-departed youth. She would like to have seen more of the place, but just now her one desire was to get away. Across the room was a door, and to this she hastened. It was locked—and no key was in the great padlock that fastened the chains. It came to her that Gaspar Cordero had fears for his life— what with heavy chains on the outer door—iron bars across his windows.

She returned to the door through which she had entered. Approaching footsteps warned her. Panic again seized her for a moment, then she heard Gaspar Cordero's voice. Another voice answered. The speaker was Cal Banning.

Anita shrank from the door, certain that she was about to be discovered—that Gaspar was bringing Banning into the room. Instead, the footsteps continued on down the corridor. She ventured to open the door a trifle and peep through, glimpsing them as they turned into the adjoining room. The brief, amazing glance told her that Banning was carrying the apparently dead or senseless body of a man.

The sight frightened, appalled her. She felt ill, depressed. Everywhere she went—were men—dying—or dead.

Anita leaned against the door, fighting off the nausea assailing her. She heard the men returning—they passed the door against which she pressed her slim, trembling body. Again she ventured a cautious look into the corridor. Gaspar and Banning were mounting the stairs. Her thoughts became a riot of confused conjectures. Why was Gaspar Cordero taking Banning upstairs? There was only one reason—the wounded Indian—Doc Spicer's dying servant—up there in that room! But why—why?

With an effort, the bewildered girl tore her mind from the problem. Now was her chance to get away—while Banning was upstairs. She darted into the corridor and into the public room of the cantina.

Eyes fastened on her curiously as she hastened toward the wide door opening on the front yard. A soft voice, close at her shoulder, halted her. She looked round with startled eyes at the speaker—a tall, lithe Mexican.

"I am Felipe Mendoza, Señorita Callahan," he said in Spanish. "Señor Cordero tells me that I am to take service with you—I and Ramon Lopez—" He gestured to another Mexican standing near him.

"Yes—yes," she answered hurriedly, recalling that she had spoken to Cordero of her desperate need of riders. "Señor Cordero will arrange the matter. It is in his hands." She gave them a sharp, appraising glance. "Has he told you that it is dangerous—working for the Cross Knife?"

The two young vaqueros exchanged looks. They seemed amused. Mendoza gestured scornfully with a slim, brown hand.

"The señorita ver' good to theenk we mus' be warn," he said in his English. He waved again. "These danger—eet is nossin' to Ramon and me."

"I think you are hired," declared the girl. For some reason she felt almost cheerful. Give her time—and a few more of these Felipes and Ramons who claimed that "these danger—eet is nossin' "—and she'd show the King Buzzard. With a smile and a nod, she hurried out to her waiting mare.

Dozing in the shade of an umbrella tree was an old Indian. He lifted his head, watching as she climbed into her saddle. He was nothing to attract the girl's attention. She was more interested in the great bay stallion tied near her chestnut mare. As she rode away, the stallion lifted his head in a soft parting nicker. The mare answered with a shrill neigh.

The old Indian watched until the girl was lost to sight, then he got to his feet and shuffled to a hammer-headed pinto. A sly glance back at the cantina door, and he was in the saddle, the pinto jogging slowly up the hill road to San Carlos.

CHAPTER XV

The stallion's parting call to the chestnut mare—
her response—told Banning what had happened.
For reasons unknown, Anita Callahan had fled.

The view from the window confirmed the
astonishing surmise. The girl was losing no time
putting distance between her and the cantina.
The mare was on the dead run up the hill road to
San Carlos. Something else he observed through
the window—the old Indian—Sassoon's man—
jogging away on his pinto horse.

Banning frowned. It might be coincidence—the
presence of the Indian—or it might mean—
Sassoon. He spoke worriedly to Cordero, now by
his side, gaping stupidly at the vanishing girl.

"That old Indian," Banning asked; "is he round
here often?"

The inn-keeper shook his head. "Seldom, Señor.
Chico mos' all time at Sassoon's cantina." He
gave the young man an anxious look. "I no
onderstan' why the señorita go so queek—no tell
me she go."

"Something frightened her," decided Banning.
"What do you suppose could have frightened her,
Cordero?"

The inn-keeper declared he couldn't imagine
what had frightened the señorita. "Perhaps the

Indian," he suggested. "She see him from window—she theenk maybe he follow her."

Banning nodded. "Whatever it was—something scared her," he repeated. He turned irresolutely toward the door. "I'm going to find out!" He was running as he threw the words back at Cordero, clattering down the hall, the sound of his booted feet fading into the distance.

The inn-keeper had not stirred from the window. He now stared down at the horses under the umbrella trees. Banning was running with the quick short step peculiar to the cowboy with his chaps and high heels. The great stallion was watching him, head flung high, forefoot stamping eagerness to be off in the chase he sensed was at hand. A twitch at the tie-rope—the slap of leather chaps against saddle, a flurry of dust as shod hoofs dug into earth—and the big bay horse was streaking up the hill.

A faint stirring from the blankets in the corner drew Cordero's gaze from the window. He stared for a moment, almost holding his breath. The wounded Piute's eyes were open—regarding him —beckoning him. Swiftly the inn-keeper moved to his side.

The Indian spoke, his voice feeble. Cordero bent over him, listened eagerly as the man spoke again. The few muttered words seemed to inexpressibly shock, startle, the innkeeper. He drew back with a low, amazed exclamation. A spasm of pain jerked across the Piute's dark, leathery face; his head fell loosely forward, eyes wide-staring.

For a long moment Cordero stood motionless, intently eyeing the still face of the Indian. His lips moved in a soundless whisper, huge hand lifting to his breast in a swiftly-fingered cross.

Again he bent down, gently drawing the blanket over the staring eyes.

There was an odd, fiercely exultant gleam in the old man's cavernous eyes as he went from the room and padded softly down the stairs. Reaching the lower floor, he went on silent feet to the little room in which Slim Dotton had been left to sleep off his indisposition. The room was empty. With an astonished grunt Cordero went quickly down the corridor and into the long, dim, patron's room.

"The gringo—where is he?" he demanded, as Ramon and Felipe, looking somewhat perplexed, hurried to him.

Felipe Mendoza jerked a thumb at the outer door. "He has this moment passed through the room—very drunk—and angry. But first—the other tall gringo ran out in great haste—is already far away—"

Cordero brushed him aside, huge bulk moving with surprising speed to the cantina door. Slim Dotton was lurching unsteadily to his horse. Cordero watched, his expression inscrutable.

The two vaqueros looked over his shoulder. Felipe spoke. "You want this gringo?" His dark eyes glittered. There was keen longing in his voice.

"Let him go," muttered the inn-keeper. "He is a sparrow—one of the sparrows." His gaze swung to their tense, swarthy faces. "At dark—we ride to the Cross Knife—" Cordero's thumb flickered up at the ceiling. "Before we ride—we dig a grave."

"The Indian—he is dead?" It was Felipe Mendoza who put the question, white teeth in a wolf-like gleam.

"He is dead," Cordero told them, "but not without his revenge." His somber gaze returned to the Double S cowboy fighting under the umbrella tree with his rearing, snorting bronco.

Slim Dotton might be drunk, his mind in a drug-stupified maze, but the feel of saddle leather between his legs seemed to have a sobering effect. The watching Cordero saw the long, lean body become one with the squealing, bucking horse as it straightened out to flash up the hill in full-striding gallop.

"He is not so drunk," muttered the inn-keeper. He seemed surprised—uneasy. Bushy brows bristling in deep thought, the old man moved quickly to the locked drawer behind the bar.

"The cantina is closed within the hour," he brusquely told the few remaining patrons. "In the meantime, amigos, Pedro will care for your wants."

After a few muttered words with his assistant, Cordero went padding on slippered feet into the hall. From one big hand dangled the silver spurs.

There was a stirring of feet in the big room, a soft whispering of voices, as the door closed him from the view of some half score pairs of curious eyes.

"The ancient one rides—then," murmured one of the men. He was a stocky, middle-aged Yaqui, with fierce eyes and coarse, grizzled hair. Throwing down a pack of greasy cards he pushed his chair back from the spindly-legged table and eyed his companions inquiringly. Like himself they were vaquero-garbed; swart, lean-waisted riders, in whose eyes could be read unmistakable fear.

As if their silence was answer enough to his wordless query, the Yaqui shrugged and turned to the door through which the inn-keeper had vanished, huge-roweled spurs scraping with a dull jangle on the earthen floor.

Chapter XVI

It was in Anita's mind to stop in San Carlos long enough to tell Asa Coons that her mind was made up—that she would rather die than accept his proposal to take over the Cross Knife and cancel Don Mike's note.

Perhaps she was foolish—but she couldn't help it. She was a Callahan. Fifty thousand dollars, he said he would give her. She could go away to some far-distant city and live in comfort—he had outrageously told her. Anita suddenly was conscious of a wave of furious anger. What was fifty thousand dollars? A bagatelle—compared with what the Cross Knife meant to a Callahan! All else aside, she wasn't at all sure of the genuineness of that note Asa Coons said was signed by Don Mike. She was inclined to be suspicious of that note. It was not the handwriting she questioned. That resembled Don Mike's bold angular scrawl closely enough. It was something else that had struck her as odd—something of small import to other people—but vastly significant to herself.

Don Mike was proud of his illustrious Pinzon blood. Anita knew that his signature invariably included the *Pinzon*—Michael Pinzon Callahan. She had been on the point of calling the banker's attention to the omission of the maternal family name in this purported signature. Something had deterred her—some instinctive caution. The more she thought of it—the more convinced she was that the whole matter was a fraud.

It seemed unbelievable that Asa Coons was that kind of a man. Greed for money had turned him crooked, she decided. Don Mike's death had somehow given him the idea of ringing in this bogus note on her. He knew that she would not dream of dishonoring her grandfather's obligation. But the schemer had tripped up on the signature.

Anita felt sick about it—assailed by ghastly doubts. How could she prove her suspicions? How could she do anything? Asa Coons would merely tell her that this had been one time when Don Mike had not used the *Pinzon* in his signature. He could claim that Don Mike was nervous—hurried, that he was not his usual self.

"He's got me," she reflected dismally. "Asa Coons has got me—unless a miracle happens."

The speedy mare flew up the long rise, with San Carlos beyond, sprawled on the mesa. From the bluffs, Anita caught a last glimpse of Old Town, huddled on the flats below. She saw something else—a great bay horse, tearing up the looping trail, rider bending low in the saddle. Cal Banning—obviously desperately determined to overtake her.

Anita forgot her half-resolution to see Asa Coons. She didn't care to see Banning. The less she saw of him the better it pleased her. She swung the mare from the road and fled across the mesa, pointing directly for El Toro's lofty peak rising majestically from the swelling uplands of the Cross Knife hacienda.

The course took her a half mile south of the town, and soon she was again back in the century-old wagon-trail leading southeast to the ranch. She ventured a backward glance. To her dismay and anger, the stallion had clung to the pursuit—was coming with the speed and sureness of an arrow. Banning was not to be shaken off.

The mare's gallant effort was no match for those powerful pistoning legs drawing ever closer. With a rush of indignation, Anita forced herself to draw rein. This wild flight was scarcely dignified, she told herself. Let the man overtake her! A lot of good it would do him. She would ignore him—for all his trouble.

A handsome bay nose thrust alongside—a sleek, white-blazed head. Anita could not resist an admiring glance. The great horse was a seasoned runner, she saw—a thoroughbred.

She rode on, lovely chin haughtily up, eyes forward, disdainful of the bay stallion's rider. Banning gave her a puzzled glance. He sensed completely that his presence annoyed her—that she had deliberately attempted to avoid him. He stole another glance. Her manner indicated that as far as she was concerned, he was not riding there by her side.

He smiled. Very well—he would seize the opportunity of frankly enjoying the charming face under the wide-brimmed white hat.

Delicate color waved into the girl's cheeks. She was unable to cope with the sustained, cool appraisal of those gray eyes; her resolve to ignore this man went by the board.

"Well!" she blazed at him; "haven't you been rude enough—forcing your company on me—that you need to stare and stare?"

"It's really the first time I've had a fair look at you," Banning told her. Abruptly he switched to his object.

"I saw you riding away from the cantina. That old Indian—Chico—seemed to be following you—and—well—that and some other things I've learned—had me worried."

"Most kind of you, I'm sure—to be worried about me." Her tone was cool, ironic.

"I wanted to tell you," he continued, flushing, "that I've been thinking about that job you offered me—"

"Please do not exercise yourself about it," she interrupted icily. "I'd quite forgotten the matter."

"I haven't forgotten it," said Banning in an annoyed voice. "I'd like the job."

"It's useless to discuss such an impossible thought," she answered. "Now that you have said your say—perhaps you will kindly ride in some other direction."

"I haven't said my say," Banning told her grimly. "You need me at the Cross Knife, Miss Callahan. I happen to know it is unsafe for you to be alone out there on the ranch."

"That is for me to say!" she answered furiously. "I'm not sure that your presence at the ranch would add to my security. I don't know you, Mr. Banning! The more I see of you—the less I like you. Is that clear to you?"

"No mistaking what you mean—if you mean what you say." The tall cowboy's gray eyes were suddenly hard. "Trouble is, Miss Callahan—you are purposely trying to hurt me." He glowered at her from his big horse. "Go on—hurt me—if it makes you feel any better. I'm repeating—you need me at the Cross Knife."

"Listen to the man," she jeered. "Knows all about women—what they mean—or don't mean!"

Despite her scorn she had flinched under his accusation. He sensed that the shaft had driven home.

"What I know about women has nothing to do with it," he grumbled. "Reckon they all have claws."

Anita hid a smile. Claws—yes—she had claws

—sharp ones. It gave her an odd satisfaction to use them on this man. Aloud, she said with an affronted laugh, "So—I'm a cat—am I? Well—you are frank—for a mere stranger." Her gaze went to him in a sideways stare. "So you have quit the Double S? Or have you been fired?" she added stingingly.

"Neither," Banning informed her. In turn he shot a question at her. "Do you trust—Sassoon?"

"Why—of course!" She gave him an amazed glance. "Not that I have any intention of discussing my friends with you."

"And Gaspar Cordero?" he persisted.

"Gaspar Cordero would die for me," Anita told him simply. For the first time he recognized sincerity in her voice.

"And Sassoon—he would do the same?" he asked.

"What business is it of yours, what Sassoon would do?" She gave him a suspicious glance. "You've heard talk at the Double S—about him —and me?"

"Some talk," admitted Banning.

Her brows puckered in a frown of distaste. It was plain she did not relish the coupling of her name with Sassoon.

"Joe Sassoon has always been a good friend," she said, unconsciously on the defensive. "The only thing I have against him is his saloon. He is too good a man for that sort of business."

"Probably—highly profitable," suggested Banning dryly. His tone was suddenly significant. "Of course—he owns a half interest in the Double S ranch."

"That's only a happen-so," she rejoined quickly, again in that same defensive manner. "He loaned Stenger money—was practically forced into the partnership. Mr. Sassoon has actually nothing to do with the way the Double S is managed—the hiring of the men. He leaves everything to Al Stenger."

"I gather that your opinion of the Double S and its doings—is not so good," commented the cowboy. His smile was grim. "Perhaps that explains your attitude toward me."

"Perhaps it does," admitted Anita. "Birds of a feather flock together. What I hear of your Double S friends only further proves that old saw. They're all of a stripe with Stenger. I wouldn't put it past him to do dirty work on the range—rustling and—" She faltered, "—and even murder. So there, Mister Banning—that should be enough for you. Unless you're just plain dumb you can easily see why there is no job for you at the Cross Knife. I simply don't hire your kind. Goodbye."

"One moment!" Banning's hand seized her bridle rein. "What would you say—if Gaspar Cordero—vouched for me?"

"What would I say?"

A ghastly, paralyzing thought occurred to Anita as she recalled that curious scene in the cantina corridor—the two men—her trusted Gaspar Cordero—and this Banning—so furtively carrying the limp body of a third man past the door behind which she had crouched. She threw her questioner a wild, frightened look.

"Why—I don't know," she stammered. "I would have taken Gaspar Cordero's word for anything—but now—I don't know. I saw you," she told Banning fiercely. "I saw you and Gaspar—with the dead man! If you don't take your hand from that bridle—I'll—" Her hand seized the short, heavy quirt dangling from her wrist.

"Dead man!" Banning grinned. "That was no dead man you saw. That was Slim Dotton. He'd followed me—to spy—" He shrugged. "We merely wanted him out of the way for a time."

The tense fingers relaxed their grip of the quirt. "I'm afraid I'm all in a muddle," she admitted in a faint voice. "That man was a Double S rider—wasn't he?"

Banning nodded.

"And you didn't want him round—while you talked to Gaspar?"

Again he nodded.

"It is very puzzling," declared Anita. Somehow she felt a vast relief. Gaspar Cordero was a rock of dependability—and this man was apparently his friend. Otherwise why should old Gaspar help him get rid of the spying Double S rider. She put the question.

"You know Gaspar, then? You are friends?"

"Never saw him before until this afternoon," Banning informed her.

She looked disappointed—again doubtful. He added quickly:

"We are more than friends. We are fighting for a common cause—Gaspar Cordero and I. Perhaps you can guess?" His tone was significant.

"The—the King Buzzard," she whispered, eyes opening wide.

His brief, grim nod told her that she had answered aright.

"If only I could believe you," she said, half to herself. She made a despairing gesture, as if belief in anything was too futile. "How can I know that—that even you might not be the King Buzzard—this monster who hides behind so much stealth—cunning!"

"You seemed to trust me—that night—at the Cross Knife," reminded Banning.

"Yes—" eyeing him intently, "—and that same night—a man was killed almost before my eyes —poor Doc Spicer—and his Indian—struck down—knifed in the back—"

"You know, then?—about the Indian?"

"Gaspar Cordero took me to him—upstairs," Anita said. She shivered. "Everywhere—men

174

being done to death. You were there—that night," she added pointedly.

"So were other men there!" Banning's voice was resentful.

"You can't blame me?" she flared.

"Do I look like a killer?" His warming smile suddenly wiped the resentment from him. "Come—take a good look at me. Do I carry the brand of a killer?"

Her own smile came—her laugh. She shook her head—which seemed to satisfy him. He leaned closer.

"Listen—Cordero will see you—soon. You can ask him about me—"

Anita's dark head nodded assent. "I am sure he will tell me—what I want to hear—about you—" She looked at him with searching, probing amber eyes. "But I—I do believe you—now!"

His smile came again, warming, inexpressibly pleased. "Then I'll be seeing you soon—about that job—" He broke off, gaze leaping apprehensively across the mesa, to the huddled roofs of San Carlos less than a mile distant.

Anita said in a startled voice, "It—it sounds like shooting! Why—it *is*—shooting—over there in town!"

Banning was already swinging the stallion into full stride. To his surprise the mare drew alongside, racing neck and neck with him. He reined to a plunging standstill.

"No!" he told the girl. "No use you coming! May be hell breaking loose over there!"

"I'm going!" Anita insisted. Her face was white, chin set in stubborn mold. "I'm going," she repeated. "I don't care if hell is breaking loose there—it may be the beginning of the end, and it's my business to be there."

"You'll only be in the way," Banning argued. "You will only make it harder. If it's what I think—you'll be riding right into their hands. Don't be a fool!"

"Oh—I think I hate you—telling me this and telling me that!" she cried, angry tears in her eyes.

The outburst left him unmoved. She could see his face set in hard, inflexible lines.

"Go on back to the ranch," he told her. "I promise to come—or send word—tonight."

Throwing him an exasperated look, Anita forced the mare around and went tearing away at headlong speed. Banning watched for a few moments, then convinced that the girl was actually pointed for the Cross Knife, he again drove his own horse recklessly across the brush-clad mesa.

Chapter XVII

Groups of men cluttered the board sidewalks of the little cow town, sullenly silent for the most part, eyeing Banning furtively as he drew rein in front of the Horsehead Bar. Other groups, less repressed with their tongues, surged in and out of the two saloons. San Carlos was teeming with riders in from the ranches to spend their pay. If it had not been for the all-pervading, ominous tenseness, Banning would have quickly catalogued the gunshots as another ordinary drunken shooting scrape. Even the three inert forms sprawled in the dust of the street, half hidden by the shifting crowd, might have meant that—and nothing more. But Banning sensed something vastly more serious. The pall of tragedy bore down clammily on the little border town. Those men lying there in the street—twisted, grotesque heaps, had not met their death in any common brawl. Tying the stallion, the tall cowboy shouldered through the milling groups for a closer view.

The face of the first man leaped at his eyes. Slim Dotton—whom he had thought asleep in Gaspar Cordero's place in Old Town. Now he was lying there lifeless, a gun clenched between stiffened fingers, a bluish hole in the sunburned forehead, hard face contorted into a mask of ferocity. He lay where he had fallen, head twisted up against the side of the wooden curb.

Banning's gaze sought the face of the man lying near Slim Dotton. Another Double S rider—a breed by the name of Cherokee. With a start of dismay he recognized the third man sprawled in the middle of the street, sightless eyes staring up at the fading evening sky. Sandy Kane—a Box B rider—one of Brodie's most trusted boys.

Banning stared, grim apprehension in his eyes. A Box B man—dead in the street—in a gunfight with Double S adherents! He fought free from the muttering, milling bystanders and hurried toward the swing doors of the Horsehead Bar. They pushed open and Asa Coons appeared, his expression ominously grave behind the dull gleam of amber spectacles. He halted, fixing his gaze on Banning as the latter shouldered up from the street.

"Terrible—terrible!" he said to the latter. "Poor Jim Brodie! A good man if there ever was one." He shook his head gloomily. "Too violent for his own good—too impulsive—headstrong!" Shaking his head, the money-lender moved down the sidewalk.

Banning felt queerly sick. Asa Coons could have meant only one thing. Jim Brodie was dead. Slowly he pushed his way through the doors.

The place was thronged, with Monte and two

assistants busy behind the long, wetly-gleaming mahogany. Among the faces that turned in his direction as he paused on the threshold, he failed to recognize those of the Double S men. The Double S men were conspicuous by their absence. Not even Stenger was visible in his favorite Saturday-night pleasure haunt.

Further back—in the deep, wide recess used for a dance floor, two girls were dancing mechanically with stiff-legged cowboy partners, to the doubtful music of squeaky fiddle and tunking guitar played by two Mexicans. A big kerosene lamp already burned in the center of the dance floor, and Banning could see the forced, bored smiles on the painted faces of the girls. One of them tittered shrilly at some witticism from her galloping cavalier. It was the usual early evening scene preceding the week-end revelry customary at the Horsehead. There was nothing to indicate that men had recently been shooting each other to death. Only the significant absence of Stenger—Stenger's followers—and covert, unfriendly glances from a group near the door. One of them put down his glass and approached him.

"Double S man—ain't you, feller?" he asked truculently.

Banning eyed him attentively. He was a skinny, bearded man, with harassed, desperate eyes, a small rancher by the name of Kettler, whose place had been raided and burned by the King Buzzard

179

gang. Kettler, however, had stubbornly ignored the warning. They could kill him—but they couldn't drive him from the little home he had carved out of the desert. He had struck water—an artesian well—a great, gushing, never-ceasing flow. He was fixed for life, with all that water to pour on his land, and he'd be damned if they'd drive him away from the first good thing he'd ever had. Banning recalled the circumstances. The Kettler raid was less than a week old. The man must know his days were numbered. The sheer terror in his eyes told that he knew it—was purposely stupifying fear-ridden nerves with the stuff Monte poured from his bottles.

"Double S man, ain't you?" repeated the man.

He was drunk—in a dangerous mood. In Banning he saw a Double S rider—a victim ready to his revengeful hand.

"What of it, mister?" Banning strove to curb his impatience. He had vital matters pulling at him—yet from this man he might gain an ally.

"You're a pack of murderers," said Kettler. His tongue was thick with liquor. "You're what Jim Brodie told Stenger—" He glared at the cowboy, work-calloused fingers fastening on the butt of an obviously new revolver in an equally new holster. Since the burning of his humble ranch buildings, Kettler had turned from ways of peace to the arts of war. The new gun was his flung-down gage of battle.

"What did Jim Brodie tell Stenger, Mr. Kettler?" queried Banning. Apparently he was looking with polite interest at the rancher; actually he was alertly watching those toil-hardened fingers squeezing over the shiny six-shooter.

The low-murmured conversation from the bar hushed as Kettler's voice rose to a screech.

"Told him that he was the King Buzzard! That's what Brodie told Stenger! Reckon that makes you one of 'em, huh? One of the King Buzzard's thievin', burnin' killers!" howled the crazed rancher. "Go for your gun, feller! I never killed a man yet—but I'm sure killin' one now!" He tugged furiously at the new gun, uttering a startled oath as the weapon remained jammed in the tight, stiff holder.

"She sure don't work so good yet, Mr. Kettler," mildly observed his intended victim. His gaze went to a tall, middle-aged man hurrying across the room from a game of solitaire. "Get him away from here, Brice," he told the newcomer in a low voice. "Put him in some safe place—or he won't last the night out."

The tall man nodded. He was a capable-appearing person. Owner of a big ranch bordering the Spanish Sinks, Bill Brice and his numerous riders were not often seen in San Carlos.

At his summoning glance, some half-score watchful-eyed men moved from the bar, surrounding the inebriated rancher still futilely tugging at his gun. A low-spoken word from Brice and the Broken Ladder men were moving into the street, the almost tearfully protesting Kettler in their midst.

Banning and the Broken Ladder owner seemed to drift into the dimmer recesses of the barroom, among the green-clothed tables, not yet ringed by faces deeply intent on the fall of the cards. There was no lamp burning here; they stood, vague, unnoticeable, in the semi-gloom, speaking in quick, low tones.

"You've heard from Ben?" Banning's voice was eager.

Brice said, "Better'n that. Ben turned up at the Broken Ladder last night—"

"He's in town with you?"

Brice shook his head. "Figured it wouldn't be safe for him to be seen round town. Got him under cover—down in the tules by Frio Creek."

"What did he find out?"

"Plenty," muttered Brice. He glanced cautiously at the bar. "Man—it's just like what you said he'd find there at the Rancho Estero!"

"So he found 'em, huh? The Cross Knife dogies?"

"I'll say he found 'em," grunted Brice. "A lot of other brands with 'em, young feller." The Broken Ladder man grinned. "There's a big trail-herd headin' back into the Sinks tonight—with Jim Blair and his Frying Pan boys on the job."

"Good old Windy Ben!" Banning's gray eyes danced.

"Windy's goin' hog wild—when he hears about Jim Brodie," said Brice.

"Things have been moving too fast for me," complained Banning. "What's happened to Brodie? Met Asa Coons outside and he hinted things—"

"Jim Brodie is dead—with Al Stenger's bullet in his heart," Brice informed him.

"How'd the gunplay start?" Banning's tone was grave—apprehensive. He went on quickly: "You know—I figured Brodie as too impulsive to be a safe man for us to take in on this deal. Was afraid he'd go off half-cocked and spill the beans. Was that the trouble, Brice? Do you think Brodie learned what we were pullin' off?"

"He didn't know nothin' of our play," Brice assured him. "Brodie and Sandy Kane came ridin' hell-bent about fifteen minutes after I moseyed in with the boys. They slam-banged into the barroom —Brodie red-eyed and cursin' the King Buzzard for handin' him the black feather. He showed it to us, yellin' his head off and swearin' no black feather'd run him off the Box B. Sassoon and Al Stenger must have heard the racket and come runnin' from the back room. Minute Brodie laid eyes on Stenger he went for him—accused him of bein' the King Buzzard. Stenger reached for his gun, and this Sandy Kane who was standin' behind Brodie, reached for his—"

The Broken Ladder man paused, swore softly. "Things sure happened fast then, Banning. A sort of triple play, it was. Stenger throwed down on Brodie—Sandy Kane behind Brodie throwin' down on Stenger, and off to one side—Slim Dotton's six-gun going into action on Sandy. Brodie dropped with Stenger's lead in his heart, and Slim's bullet swung Sandy round but didn't drop him. He was sure game—that Box B rannihan. His gun smokin'—he followed Slim Dotton into the street and drilled him in the head. Slim's bunkie turned loose then and dropped old Sandy. Sandy had one second to live and one bullet to give away. He gave it to the hombre that got him. That's the story, Banning. Four dead men inside of five seconds. Had all I could do to keep my boys under control. Knew it wasn't time to act. Couldn't start nothin' without your say-so."

"Brice," said the younger man grimly. "If things break right—we'll clean up tonight. Brodie's killin' means the King Buzzard gang visits the Box B before morning. We'll be ready for them. They'll try to work fast—sweep the range clean of those Box B dogies." His quick glance swept the room. "Where's Stenger—and the outfit?"

"Sassoon bawled Stenger out for the shootin'.

Stenger got sore—took his outfit across the street to Dutch Jake's place." The Broken Ladder man broke off. "There's Sassoon now," he muttered. "Reckon we'd better not let him see us talkin' too friendly."

They drifted casually across the room. "Pick up Ben Allen and get your outfit movin' for the Box B," Banning said in a low voice. "Aim to make it there soon after dark. You know the place—down there on the Little Anita."

Brice nodded, sauntered on toward the swing doors. Sassoon, framed in his office entrance, gave him a sharp, glittering glance.

"What were you and Bill Brice whispering about?" he demanded suspiciously as Banning approached.

"Was that the feller's name?" Banning's voice was indifferent. "Why—that crazy jasper—Kettler—made a play for me when I come in. Damned me for another of Stenger's hired killers and went for his gun. This here feller—Brice, you call him—had his boys throw him out. We got to talkin' about this Brodie killin'."

Sassoon's face darkened. "Bad business," he grumbled. "Not that Brodie wasn't to blame—calling Al what he did."

Banning nodded. "Sure had no business accusin' Stenger of being the King Buzzard," he agreed. "Can't say I blame Al for shootin' him up. What's the idea—leavin' them others lay out in the street—Slim Dotton and Cherokee—and that Box B jasper?"

"Ace Coons," Sassoon told him sourly. "He's sore as a boil. Says he's sending for a deputy marshal from Santos and don't want the bodies touched. Swears Stenger has got to stand trial."

Banning grinned. "Reckon Stenger has nothin' to be scared of. Reckon there's too many witnesses to swear that Brodie started the trouble. So Al got cold feet, huh? High-tailed it back to the ranch, huh?"

Sassoon shook his head. "You'll find him and the boys over at Dutch Jake's place. I ran 'em out of the Horsehead. Was afraid of more trouble."

"What's been done with Brodie?" Banning's tone was casual.

"In here." Sassoon opened the office door. "Want to see him?"

He closed the door behind them, watching the cowboy keenly as the latter stared down at the still form lying on the horsehair sofa. At that moment, Sassoon's expression was the vicious snarl of a great cat stalking an unsuspecting victim.

In Banning's eyes was a sudden fleeting hot anger as he gazed in silence at the slain owner of the Box B. With an effort he forced himself to a brutal, callous comment.

"Stenger sure fixed him proper," he said, turning a grin on the other man. "Well—ain't my funeral. Don't interest me none—viewin' the sad remains."

"That's the way with you professional killers," reproved Sassoon. "No respect for death." He changed the subject abruptly.

"So you didn't get the spurs, eh? Old Cordero wouldn't make a deal, Slim Dotton was telling Stenger and me."

"Was that all Slim told you?" Banning's voice was innocent. "Didn't he tell you how he got pie-eyed on Cordero's red wine?" Banning shook his head solemnly. "Sure give me a start—seein' old Slim layin' dead out in the street! Thought I'd left him snorin' down in the cantina."

Sassoon seemed confused for a moment, irritated. "Maybe not so drunk at that. Slim was always one to sober up fast." His voice grew soft, purring. "Slim said he saw you riding up on the mesa with the Callahan girl."

"Tell you what I think," declared Banning angrily; "Stenger sent Slim trailin' me down in Old Town. Sure don't like Stenger settin' spies on me that way. I'm lopin' right over to Dutch Jake's and bawl Al out good and plenty. That sort of play don't sit well with me."

"Not a bad idea," agreed Sassoon. "Stenger will be wondering where you've got to." He eyed the black-handled guns in Banning's holster. "He'll be needing you, feller—you and your guns. That's what he hired you for."

He followed the cowboy out to the barroom, Banning again vowing he would take Stenger to task for his sly espionage. Sassoon shrugged, turned to the bar, eyes signaling the old Indian.

"Follow him," he told Chico in an undertone. He nodded at the tall figure pushing through the swing doors. "If he leaves town—tell me at once."

The Indian went swiftly into the street. Sassoon waited, eyes fixed on the door; long, slim fingers drumming nervously on the polished bar. In a minute or two, the Indian reappeared.

"Him go Dutch Jake's," he informed Sassoon briefly.

The saloon man nodded, a glitter of satisfaction in his black eyes. He pondered for a moment.

"Chico," he said suddenly. "Get my black horse—have him waiting out at the back door."

The Indian sped away. Sassoon's gaze went sifting through the faces thronging the bar. One by one, several men detached themselves from the crowd in response to his beckoning eyes. Unobserved, singly and in couples, they drifted into the street. They were a singularly hard-faced lot, and not a man among them but wore a gun slung low on either thigh. Sassoon smiled grimly—sauntered back to the office, pausing to speak to the white-aproned Monte.

"If anybody asks for me—I'm at the Double S for over Sunday," he told the bartender.

"Checking up accounts with Stenger," he added with a thin smile. "That gunplay of his fixed him with me, Monte. We're through as partners in the Double S ranch. He'll buy me out—or sell out to me." Sassoon eyed the bartender slyly. "Get me, Monte?" he asked.

"I git yuh, boss." The bartender grinned. "If any of these nosey gents comes askin' for yuh tonight—I'll spill what yuh told me—" He wagged his head. "Sure—yuh've done gone to the ranch to have it out with Al Stenger. Yuh're on the prod with him an' aims to dissolve the bonds of yore pardnership pronto."

"That's the play, Monte." Giving the man a sinister smile, Sassoon disappeared into the office.

Chapter XVIII

Vague fears oppressed Anita as she rode into the ranch yard. The place seemed so deserted, so ominously lacking in the usual throbbing stir of life as she knew it on the Cross Knife. The great corrals, once echoing the bawls of newly-weaned calves, and the stampings and snorts of the roundup cavvy, struck her as vast and lonesome pools of moonlight, peopled with shadowy, fearsome things that moved around her on silent, thronging feet; terrifying shapes, ghosts of murdered men—shades of their murderers, watching with mocking, pitiless eyes.

The weary ride in from San Carlos had found her at the Big Anita, the sun long since down, and Callahan's Crossing mantled in blackness. For nearly an hour she had been forced to wait on the wrong side of the darkly sullen stream, until at last the lifting moon had spread its silvery path from bank to bank. She had crossed, then, careful to keep the mare's nose pointed toward the gap in the cedar brakes on the opposite shore. Callahan's Crossing was a straight and narrow path—with slimy death on either hand for reckless man or beast.

Callahan's Crossing had completely undone her. The long wait in the loneliness and the darkness, and the racking hours of the afternoon, had left Anita feeling drained of courage and strength. The sight of the towering trees closing in the old ranch house sent shivers through her. They were like monstrous, moaning giants, agleam with elfin candlelight, for the luring of unsuspecting mortals into the treacherous embrace of their darkly-reaching arms. It was a foolish thought, Anita told herself. Her nerves were shredded raw, betraying her to silly fancies. She forced herself from the saddle.

How ghastly quiet it was—and where was Pio? Why wasn't he there to take her horse? She cried his name, her voice seeming absurdly tiny in that vast, moonlit stillness.

No answer! No sound of hastening feet! Only silence!

Anita was suddenly horribly, utterly afraid. She clung to the bridle reins, knees weak, trembling. What did it mean? Where was Pio? Where were the others—the pitifully few vaqueros Clem had persuaded to fill the vacancies left by her murdered riders? For that matter—where was Clem Sanders? Her frightened, tense gaze went to the rambling old house beyond the high-walled garden. Darkness there—only darkness!

Desperately she fought away the horror closing over her, stifling her. There was a reason—of course there was a reason. Clem had the vaqueros somewhere out on the range—had not returned.

So she reassured herself outwardly, yet inwardly aware that she had not explained away this grim silence—the lack of lamplit windows. There were servants in the house or had been—when she left for San Carlos.

The mare's eyes reproached her. Chita was tired—impatient for her stall. Nothing, just then, could have forced Anita into that dark cavernous building. She saw that the doors were open. With icy fingers she loosened saddle-cinch and bridle, throwing them across the top rail of the corral fence. The mare shook herself, went nosing the ground before proceeding to enjoy the luxury of a roll in the soft dust. Anita lingered, pretending to watch the mare's gyrations. She dreaded going to the house.

The mare finished her dust bath and continued on to the stables. Anita was suddenly panicky. She wanted to run after the mare. At least Chita was company—was something alive—real. She grew angry with herself. She was acting like a little fool—like a plain, everyday coward!

She fairly whipped herself through that corral gate. Presently the high heels of her little boots went clicking smartly along the stone walk of the flower-scented patio. She took no further pause for apprehensive thought, fearing that to delay would weaken her nerve. Despite her resolve, her feet lagged as they neared the wide corridor. She could hear the quick beating—the hammering of her heart. It was the only sound she could hear—that—and the night wind moaning through the trees.

The wide patio door was open. Moonlight filtered like silver spray through the oriole window over the great front entrance down at the far end of the long hall. She went inside, driving the lagging feet, and fumbled matches from the silver box on a side table. She struck one, and in a moment the big swinging lamp was sending out its white, revealing glow.

The friendly flame reassured her. She found strength, comfort, in the familiar surroundings. The great hall of her ancestors. They gazed down at her from painted canvas—brave, stately men—brave, lovely women; they were there with her in spirit—the Pinzons and the Callahans.

Anita's gaze went from portrait to portrait, to rest finally on the latest and last to be hung on those paneled oak walls. Her own—completed within the year.

There was something queer there—something stuck in the frame across the white oval of the painted cheek. Anita was sure her heart had forever stopped its beating. The blood drained from her face, leaving it a frozen, white mask of horror. That thing there on her portrait—that thing—was a *black feather.*

Blindly, with shaking hand, she groped for a chair. "Mustn't faint," she told herself. "Must keep my—my head." She collapsed into the chair's yielding depths—lay there—very still, eyes closed, long curling lashes startlingly black and beautiful against damask skin. She began to shudder. Her heart was racing now, stifling her with thunderous pulsations. She felt very queer. She was going to have a stroke, she thought dully. Once, one of the kitchen women had had a stroke. Anita remembered her feeling of helplessness. The woman had looked so dead—so completely gone from life.

The dizziness left her presently. Her heart was something like its normal self again. She found she could think without that overwhelming horror interfering with the processes of mind and reason. The first thing to do, Anita decided, was to conquer this devastating fear—force herself to face coolly this sinister thing that had come to her. She would count three—and then open her eyes.

Aloud, she said slowly—"One . . . two . . . *three*." Her long, dark lashes lifted—she stared deliberately at the portrait—at the little black feather lying across the curve of rose-flushed cheek. She continued to look at it steadily, letting her healthy young body relax, letting her mind resume its usual orderliness and composure. First she thought of Clem Sanders. There were only two things she could think about him. Either he was away on some ranch business—his return delayed—or he was somewhere nearby—dead.

She knew that if Clem had come in since the warning of the black feather, he would not have left it there for her to see. Of that Anita was certain. On the other hand, there may have been an encounter—with the result that poor Clem had died in vain for her. As for the vaqueros—the servants—it was not hard to understand about them. Sheer terror would have scattered them to the four winds. Recent events at the Cross Knife were too fresh in their minds to allow them to remain in the shadowed path of the dead King Buzzard.

Next, she found herself thinking of Cal Banning—the mysterious stranger from nowhere. At least, he was mysterious to her. She wondered about him. He had promised to come to her tonight—or to send word.

She hoped he wouldn't send word. She hoped that he would come in person—riding into the yard on that great bay stallion. There was something extraordinarily capable about him. There was power and force in that long, lean, finely-drawn body of his, and courage—cool efficiency in the alert gray eyes. She had thought so that terrible night now nearly two weeks away. She had found herself instinctively turning to him, even then—instead of to good old Jim Brodie—or Sassoon. His refusal to quit the Double S for the Cross Knife, despite her almost hysterical appeal, had hurt her tremendously.

She realized now why she had so bitterly condemned him—accused him in her mind of the most awful things. Anita's face went suddenly hot. She had been perfectly terrible—an absolute vixon. His patience had been amazing. It was a wonder he hadn't left her and her troubles flat. It wouldn't have been any more than she deserved —jumping to ugly conclusions because she was mad at him.

A smile curved the girl's lips. For the moment she forgot that ominous black thing stuck in the frame of her portrait. She was thinking of the devil-may-care tilt of that old black Stetson on Cal Banning's well-shaped head. His hair was so crisply thick—dark—almost black, with a tinge of red that visibly deepened when the sunlight struck it. Almost like Don Mike's might have been when he was a young man.

An impulse lifted Anita from the big chair. There was a portrait of Don Mike among those others hanging on the dark paneled walls. For generations it had been a custom for each member of the family to be done in oils upon reaching adult age. Don Mike's was the fourth from her own, next to her grandmother. Between hers and her grandmother's hung those of her father, the little Don Mike—in his early twenties, and his wife, her young mother.

Oblivious still of the black feather, she went to the fourth picture—Don Mike—on his twenty-first birthday. Yes—he had the same reddish-black hair—Cal Banning's hair. Anita studied the lean hawk's face critically. There was something oddly similar about the mouth—the nose though, was not so strongly arched as Cal Banning's. But the eyes were the same gray eyes, coolly alert. It was really remarkable, she told herself excitedly. She must call Cal Banning's attention to the resemblance.

Her gaze came back to her own portrait, eyes dilating as they rested on that hideous black thing there on the frame. She made a movement to snatch it away. A second thought restrained her. She would leave it there. It would be her gage of battle to the unknown killer. Yes—it would be—just that!

In spite of her bold resolution, Anita was conscious now of her unprotected state. There were guns in the house, she knew. From now on she would keep a gun handy—carry one day and night. Somewhat timidly she went down the hall to the gun-case near the front door, a great, carved cabinet of black oak.

She looked through the glass doors, mentally selecting from among the array of weapons. There was one she liked—a slim, long, beautifully mounted .38. She opened the doors and took it down, with its holster of finely-worked Mexican leather. It was loaded, she saw, with cartridges in the belt. Smiling faintly, she buckled the holster round her slim waist and slipped fingers over the smooth ivory handle of the gun. Unconsciously the fingers tightened with a fierce, startled grip. She spun on her heels, lithe young body tense, eyes and ears alert. The sound was unmistakable! The crunching of hoofs on the sandy drive winding through the trees! Horsemen—several of them!

For a moment, Anita's heart beat a rapid tattoo. She was frightened—horribly frightened. And then she remembered. Cal Banning—of course! He had kept his promise—had arrived at last.

Relieved, she went to the patio door—stood there, waiting, listening.

The riders were in the corral, now. She heard voices, and presently a tall figure strode with a jingling of spurs along the narrow stone corridor leading into the patio; a figure, vague, indistinct, in the misty moonlight. Of course it was Cal Banning, Anita reassured herself.

She stepped outside, stood there, framed against the mellow lamplight. The tall figure drew near—Anita uttered a startled little cry.

The man coming toward her across the patio was not Cal Banning. For some reason, fear came to her again, left her feeling sick. It was Sassoon—striding toward her through the moonlight. Sassoon—from San Carlos!

Chapter XIX

The same moon that lighted Anita Callahan safely over the treacherous crossing of the Big Anita River, saw some twenty horsemen jogging along the sandy floor of a dry wash. There was something grimly business-like in the way they rode, wordless, furtively-alert. They progressed with a dearth of sound—a soft, muffled beat of hoofs on sand, an occasional tinkle of spur and creak of saddle leather.

The big red-haired man riding at the head of the column leered at his companion.

"Soon be thar, Banning. The Box B ain't fur, now. We'll be seein' the house round that thar next bend."

Even in the moonlight, Banning's face showed harassed, tense lines. It had not been his plan to find himself riding for the Box B with the Double S outfit.

When he left Sassoon in the Horsehead Bar with the avowed intention of searching out Stenger in Dutch Jake's place, it had been his secret purpose to make a stealthy and hurried departure for the Cross Knife. A chance glance had warned him that Sassoon's Indian was slyly watching. Careful not to betray to the spy that he had been observed, Banning had reluctantly entered Dutch Jake's saloon. A false move at this time would arouse Sassoon's suspicions, he reasoned. He realized that an attempt to leave town would bring on a crisis dangerous to the plans he had risked his life to arrange.

Stenger met him with every evidence of jovial friendship, immediately calling for the bartender to set up the drinks.

For a man who had recently shot a fellow-being to death, the red-headed cattleman seemed in a hilarious mood.

"Yuh're just in time, feller," he told Banning. "Soon's we have drunk 'er down we're ridin'." He winked. "Right in yore line, feller."

"About time you was showin' me some excitement," Banning grinned knowingly. "What's the play, Stenger? Sassoon sort of tipped me off that things were movin' fast tonight."

Stenger's face went black. "Huh? What was Sassoon tellin' yuh, Banning?"

"Something about some Box B dogies," said the cowboy. "Told me to look you up pronto. Kind of hinted my guns maybe would be smokin' right soon."

Stenger seemed relieved. He burst into a loud laugh, leaned close to Banning. "So Joe Sassoon figgers himself in on this deal, huh? Listen, Cal—me an' Sassoon is through. I ain't pardners with a man that bawls me out like he done. Jim Brodie had it comin'—namin' me what he did." Stenger drained his glass and slammed it on the bar. "I'll tell yuh about them Box B dogies. Seems Sassoon made a deal with Brodie just before the shootin'— buys the Brodie Box B spread—lock, stock an' barrel. Seems Brodie was fixin' to leave the Sinks for good, on account of the King Buzzard handin' him the black feather—" The cattleman grinned. "Well, feller—Sassoon ain't gettin' them steers. To hell with him an' that sanctified Ace Coons— threatenin' to have the law on me—have me stretchin' hemp! I'm beatin' them coyotes to it, Cal. The boys is with me to the last man. We're rustlin' them Box B dogies tonight—pushin' em through Lobo Pass into Old Mexico. Reckon we'll have the laugh on Sassoon and Coons once we get below the line, huh?"

"Looks that way," agreed the cowboy. He hesitated. "Reckon I won't be ridin' with you, Al. Kind of suits me down here in the Sinks." He grinned. "There's reason why it ain't so healthy for me—down below the line."

There was a snarl on the cattleman's liquor-inflamed face. "No time to quit me now, Banning," he said grimly. "I'd be a fool to leave you loose here—maybe runnin' to Sassoon with what I told yuh confidential."

"Don't worry me none—what you do to Sassoon," retorted Banning. "I'm just telling you that this play of yours don't enthuse me. I hired out to the Double S and it seems you're kissin'

201

the ranch *adios* and seekin' new pastures. Reckon that breaks our contract, Stenger. Here's where you and I part company." Banning's hands slid casually to the black butts of his guns.

"Mister," said Stenger softly. "Listen to me. We ain't partin' company like yuh says. Look round, feller—you've got good eyes—an' they ain't tellin' yuh wrong."

"Sure I've got good eyes," drawled the young man. "I've already spotted those three gunmen of yours in the mirror—ready to plug me in the back. And while I'm talkin', Stenger, I'm telling you I've got more brains than you give me credit for havin'. You've got a hard-lookin' bunch of hombres mixed in here with your outfit. Where'd they come from—these gun-slingers? Seem mighty friendly with your boys."

Stenger was watching him craftily, obviously puzzled by Banning's cool sarcasm. "What yuh drivin' at?" he demanded gruffly.

Banning grinned. "You know as well as I do that Dutch Jake don't own this booze joint. You and I know what most folks don't—that Sassoon owns the Palace Bar." He grinned again as Stenger gave him a startled look. "That being true—let's lay our cards on the table—"

Banning paused, steely gray eyes boring the other man. "Stenger," he said softly, "you ain't quittin' Sassoon. Your talk hasn't fooled me a moment. Stenger—what would you say if I claim

Jim Brodie came mighty close to the truth over there in the Horsehead? What would you say if I tell you to your face that we're riding tonight for the King Buzzard?"

The Double S man glared at him venomously. Banning's eyes danced. He said reproachfully:

"Sure got me sore—stringin' me along the way you done, Stenger. Time you let me in on the play—if I'm ridin' with you."

Stenger eyed him searchingly. Apparently satisfied, he nodded grimly.

"We're ridin' now," he said. His voice rose above the clamor. "All set, boys. Let's be movin'."

They stamped noisily into the street—some twenty-odd men—all Double S riders, Banning observed with some surprise and apprehension. The fact that none of the score or more hard-faced strangers accompanied them secretly disturbed him. He found himself wondering for what sinister purpose they had been left behind in Dutch Jake's Palace Bar.

With Stenger and Banning forming the spearhead, the column of horsemen rode in silence out of the town, thrusting across the desert, now mantled with twilight's deepening purple and gold. Banning's covert glances gave him another disturbing fact. Pressing closely behind Stenger and himself were three of the outfit's fastest gunmen, hands resting on the six-shooters in their belts. The derision in their hard eyes was unmistakable—told Banning that he was virtually a prisoner. He thought dismally of his promise to Anita Callahan. What would she think of his failure to appear at the Cross Knife?

Moonlight found them following the twistings of the dry wash that was to bring them close to the Box B ranch. Once, Banning thought he glimpsed a column of riders topping a rise far to the left—vague, ghostly shadows that quickly melted into the shimmering moonlight.

Ugly doubts assailed him. Brice and his men would not be coming in from that direction. What did those mysterious horsemen portend? Mentally he calculated distances. It was obvious they were not heading for the Box B. A sickening certainty rushed over him—a certainty that the ghostly riders he had glimpsed were headed for Callahan's Crossing. Like a fool he had allowed himself to fall into a cunning trap—leaving Anita Callahan to the deviltry of the King Buzzard and his killers.

As from a far distance he heard Stenger's voice.

"We'll be seein' the house soon—round that next bend—"

The outlaw's leering glance slid to the three men behind, and on the instant Banning felt the hard muzzle of a gun pressing against his spine.

There was a sudden stillness as the line of horsemen halted. Banning slowly put up his hands, inwardly steeling himself for the crashing blow of lead tearing through flesh and bone. In front of him a gray shape slunk across the silvery sandy floor of the dry wash. A coyote. From behind him sounded the mournful hoot of an owl. He found himself listening tensely. There was something peculiar about that owl, he thought.

"I'm takin' yore guns, Banning," Stenger was saying in a sneering voice. "Thought yuh had us fooled, huh?" He laughed harshly. "We're on to yuh. By rights I orter leave you layin' here for the buzzards." He leaned over—plucked out the black-handled guns and flung them into the brush. One of the men seized his hands, jerked them back—bound them tightly with a piece of rawhide.

"All set, boys," said Stenger. "Get movin'." He put his horse in motion, swinging up the bank. They followed, a man riding on either side of the prisoner. Again came the mournful call of the owl somewhere behind them. Or was it an owl? A fantastic thought surged into Banning's mind; he fastened on to it, as a man, drowning, clutches to the forlorn hope of the straw in his fingers.

Chapter XX

Lights twinkled in front of them. The Box B ranch house. For the first time, Banning remembered Nell Brodie—still ignorant of the fate that had overtaken her father. Nell Brodie—Clem Sanders' pretty fair-haired sweetheart—patiently waiting the return of the father she would never again see in this life!

It was likely that Jim Brodie had not told her of the warning he had received. She would be unaware of the impending raid—would fall into the merciless hands of the gang like a sweet ripe peach from a tree.

Banning's thoughts went to Smoky Kile. The swarthy Double S foreman had not accompanied the outfit into San Carlos for the weekly spree. He recalled now that Smoky had mysteriously disappeared earlier in the day. He had carefully shaved and slicked his black hair—had donned his best cowboy finery.

Instantly Banning knew now why Smoky Kile had foregone the pleasures of San Carlos. The Box B had been his goal—with the fair-haired Nell the lure. Smoky had known what was coming off—laid his plans accordingly. Perhaps by now he was across the border with his stolen bride.

The lighted ranch house windows indicated that

Banning's surmise was wrong—that Nell Brodie was home. From somewhere in the distance came the bawling of cattle. Banning knew the portent of that sound. The Box B cattle had already been rounded up, ready for the drive through Lobo Pass. Traitors in Jim Brodie's outfit had made ready for the raid—perhaps slain the loyal riders, or the latter may have fled before the dread shadow of the King Buzzard. Banning discarded the latter theory. Brodie had some good men in his outfit—men of the kind who put loyalty before life. They were either dead—or prisoners.

The ranch buildings loomed distinctly in the moonlight now. The big barn, set back in the corrals, some outhouses, and the small ranch house with its little garden and shading fruit trees.

There was nothing of the ancestral Cross Knife hacienda about the Box B. The home of the Brodies was typical of the rugged pioneer days of the southwest cattle country.

Not a sound came from the little house as the column of riders swung into the yard. Silently the raiders eyed the lighted windows. Stenger's voice broke the silence.

"Try the door, one of you boys," he ordered. "Reckon Smoky's busy makin' love to his gal and plumb forgot we was ridin' this way tonight."

The men snickered. One of them spurred up to the steps—hammered on the door with his gun. In vain they listened for an answering voice—the stirring of feet. Only the monotonous bawling of the Box B herd disturbed the quiet.

Stenger muttered an astonished oath. "Take a look inside, Fargo," he called to the cowboy. "Bust the door down—if she's locked."

The man swung from the saddle and warily mounted the steps. The door was not locked. He kicked it open—peered into the lighted parlor.

"Well—is Smoky there—or ain't he?" called Stenger impatiently, as the cowboy continued to stare into the room.

Fargo turned his head and looked at them stupidly. "Sure he's in there," he told them in a curiously hushed voice. "Sure Smoky is in there—layin' on the floor—daid."

Stenger uttered a startled, shocked oath—spurred to the door and leaped from the saddle. His riders surged after him, with Banning pocketed between his guards. He glimpsed a vista of the room. The place was virtually a wreck. Chairs splintered—tables overturned, broken dishes littering the floor, and, sprawled in a corner, the limp body of Smoky Kile.

Followed by several of the men, Stenger rushed into the room—bent over the still body of his late foreman. He straightened up—eyed round at the others.

"Been an awful scrap," he told them. "Smoky's face is sure battered up plenty—"

"Was hot lead that did for him," observed Fargo. He pointed to the ominous red blotch staining the front of the dead man's fancy blue-and-white silk shirt. "Drilled through the heart," he added.

Stenger growled an oath. "That means him an' Clem Sanders tangled," he declared. "Ain't hard to figger out this killin'. Clem Sanders finds Smoky makin' love to the Brodie gal—an' jumps him." He gestured at the wreckage. "Must have been a bear of a scrap until Clem gets a gun and fills Smoky with hot lead—" Stenger paused, glowered round the little parlor. "Maybe it was the gal that plugged Smoky!" He clattered across the floor. "Come on, fellers! If she's hidin' round—we'll sure fix her pronto."

Helpless between his watchful guards, Banning sat tense and white on the bay stallion, listening to the hoarse shouts, the stamp of hurrying booted feet as the gang spread like wolves through the house.

"Made her getaway," he heard Stenger grumble. The big man came lurching out, pausing on the steps until the last of the searchers straggled through the door.

"All out, boys?" Stenger lifted his gun. "Nothin' we can do for poor Smoky 'cept give him a funeral," he said grimly. The six-gun in his hand roared twice and the big swinging lamp burst into a geyser of spattering, flaming oil that fed hungrily on the flimsy window curtains—spreading like devouring red serpents up the papered walls.

For a moment Stenger stared at the inferno he had caused, the red glare lighting his savage face. He slowly pushed the gun into its holster, his bitter gaze coming round and fastening on the prisoner.

"Why don't yuh gun him down?" growled one of the outlaws. "Throw his carcass in there to keep old Smoky comp'ny?"

"I've a mind to," muttered Stenger. "I've a mind to toss the skunk in there alive." He glared murderously. "Made out he was a hunted killer—come wormin' like a snake into our bus'ness. Thought he was smart." Stenger chuckled. "Banning—yuh sure set yore own trap. Yuh come into the Sinks with yore story about bein' a hunted outlaw—an' yuh'll swing as such. That's why I ain't killin' yuh here an' now. When yuh die, feller—yuh'll die branded as the King Buzzard—terror of the Spanish Sinks—snagged red-handed by good old Stenger's Double S boys."

There was a laugh from the listening riders. Stenger continued gleefully:

"This is the last night the King Buzzard flies, Banning. Come mornin'—yuh'll be the King Buzzard—with a rope round yore neck—an' plenty hands to pull yuh up danglin'."

"Trying to make me believe you are the King Buzzard, ain't you, Stenger?" Banning said coolly.

"No such thing," denied the outlaw. "I'm declarin' right now that I don't know who is the King Buzzard—no more than these boys does. The King Buzzard's never showed us his face. Ain't that the truth, fellers?" He appealed to the clustered riders.

They nodded. "Sure is, boss," murmured one of the guards. He grinned malevolently at the prisoner. "Reckon this maverick will fit the name well as the next man."

Stenger's gaze fastened on a low building built of adobe bricks and stone, inset with a narrow, heavy door. "That there old milk-house will make a handy jail, fellers. Pull him off that horse and shove him inside. Tie his legs good," he added.

"Needn't pull me down," Banning told them quietly. He slid from the saddle. Hands seized him—pushed him roughly to the milk-house some twenty feet away. One of the men bent down to tie his ankles.

"Can use that bay horse myself," he heard Stenger tell his men.

Banning twisted his head—saw that the man had the big stallion by the bridle and was in the act of swinging into the saddle. With a squeal of fury, the great stallion reared, forefeet slashing at the would-be rider. Stenger dodged, missing death by a hair. The stallion whirled, long teeth bared, reaching for a cowboy who had attempted to seize the dropped reins. The man flung to one side and the enraged animal tore away, nostrils blowing defiance, long tail plumed high. Stenger watched, vicious-eyed, gasping for breath.

"Let him go," he rasped, as several of the men prepared to give chase. "He'll wait. Ain't got time to fool with the devil now." He turned to his own horse. "Come on, fellers. We've got to work fast."

The fire was spreading fast through the little ranch house. Tongues of flame licked over the sun-baked shingles—billowed from the windows, throwing a lurid glare over the fierce faces of the outlaws. It was Banning's last glimpse of them. With a kick and a curse, his guards thrust him headlong into the dense darkness of the milk-house. He heard the heavy door slam—the sound of the iron bolt driving into the socket.

Chapter XXI

Banning lay where he had fallen, the hard earthen floor cooling to his sweat-drenched body. From beyond the thick adobe walls of the milk-house, faintly came the roar and crackle of flames. Something else he heard—the stifled, gasping breaths of something lying near him in the blackness of that vault-like room.

A cold prickle ran down Banning's spine. He listened, holding his own breath. Again he heard the sound. The answer came to him. He sat up—peered into the darkness—spoke softly.

"That you—Miss Brodie?"

There was a faint stir—another stifled, startled gasp. He spoke again. "Don't get scared. This is Cal Banning. You remember me?"

"Oh, yes—yes," answered a girl's voice in a frightened whisper. "Oh, Mr. Banning—I've been so scared—"

"Wait a second," he told her. "Can you see me? They threw me in here—tied hand and foot."

He heard her crawling toward him—her hand touched his boot. The contact startled her; she gasped, snatching her hand away.

"That's me," he assured her. "Now see what you can do to these knots round my wrists. I'll tend to the leg ropes myself." He leaned forward, holding out his bound hands. Hers groped closer, fingers running over his hands until they came to the buckskin thongs. She set to work on the knots and presently the cords fell from his wrists.

"*Bueno*," muttered Banning. He waited for a moment, stretching the cramp out of his fingers before reaching for the cord binding his ankles. A sharp tussle with the tight knots—he was free of his bonds.

"Where's Clem?" he whispered.

"In here," came her answer. "Oh, Mr. Banning —I'm afraid he's dying!"

"Now I wouldn't say that," he soothed. "Clem is too tough to go dyin' so young."

"It was terrible," she went on. "That Smoky Kile—he—he came. I was alone. Dad's in town. Smoky was awful—tried to make me go away with him. He—he said the King Buzzard was coming to get Dad if I didn't go with him—" She paused.

"Yes?" encouraged Banning. "And then Clem— showed up—"

"They fought something awful." The girl shuddered. "Smoky got his gun out and shot Clem. I—I kicked the gun from his hand—gave it to Clem. He killed Smoky—" Her voice broke. "Clem fainted away," she added.

"Reckon I know the rest," Banning said. "You heard us ridin' in—did the only thing you could do—dragged Clem into this place—" Banning's voice was admiring. "That sure was smart of you, Miss Brodie. They figured you both got clean away."

"They've set fire to the house, haven't they?" she asked in a shaky voice. "I—I saw the flames—when the door opened. Poor dad—he'll feel dreadful!"

"Here—take my hand and sort of trail me over to where Clem's lying," said Banning, suddenly anxious to change the subject.

"Listen!" She spoke in a frightened whisper. "Somebody is coming to the door!"

The sound was unmistakable. Footsteps—the heavy bolt grating in the socket.

"Back to the wall—quick!" hissed Banning. He crouched, arms extended, ready for a plunging tackle.

A slit of moonlight—the red glare of the fire—the door swung open. Instead of plunging at the figure framed there against the crimson glow, Banning straightened up with a joyful cry.

"Cordero! So it *was* you—hootin' like an owl back there in the dry wash!"

"*Si*, Señor. We were making for the Cross Knife—when we cut your trail—saw them make you preesnor. We follow—Ramon—and the others. We watch—wait till they ride away—and now Señor—you are no more preesnor."

Cordero's gaze was on the girl crouching in the corner by the prostrate Clem Sanders, now

215

visible in the flooding light. "So—you are not alone, Señor!"

"Got a sick man here," Banning answered. He turned and bent over the wounded Cross Knife foreman.

"He's opening his eyes," whispered the girl. "Clem—Clem—" She touched him tenderly. "It's all right, Clem."

"Let's take a look at him." Banning ran expert fingers through the foreman's thick, sandy hair. He gave the girl a surprised, relieved glance. "Why—he ain't hurt serious! Smoky's bullet creased him—didn't more than slit his darned old scalp!"

"I'll get some water!" Nell exclaimed. In a twinkling she lifted a wooden pail from a shelf and placed a dipper of the cool water to Clem's lips.

"He'll be himself in a minute or two," Banning assured her. "Don't need me to help you fix him up."

He gestured to the old inn-keeper. The latter followed him outside. "Cordero," said the cowboy in a low tone. "There's trouble due at the Cross Knife! We've got to ride fast—" He broke off, ran past the side of the milk-house, putting fingers to lips. A shrill neigh answered his whistle; the big stallion came trotting into the flame-lit scene—pushed velvety nose into his master's hand.

Cordero spoke anxiously. "The señor—he spik

of mooch danger at the hacienda," he reminded.

Banning gave him a haggard look. "We haven't a chance to make it in time," he worried. "Callahan's Crossing is miles out of our way—"

Cordero interrupted him. "No, Señor. We are not so far from the hacienda—if we take the short cut. Not many know these Devil's Bridge; it ees ver' dangerous—but it remove many miles. In my youth these Devil's Bridge was nossin' to me—" Cordero smiled grimly. "Tonight—I will show you these Devil's Bridge, Señor."

"Where are your men?" demanded Banning. He was in a fever to be in the saddle.

"They keep the look-out," Cordero told him. "I will call them." From his lips came the mournful cry of an owl. Answering cries came back to them. "Soon they come," said Cordero.

For the first time, Banning noticed that the former majordomo of the Cross Knife was garbed in the splendid trappings of his youth. From boot heels gleamed the long silver spurs given him by the young mother of Anita's grandfather. Intuitively Banning sensed that this amazing centenarian had ridden forth tonight prepared to die as he had lived—a gallant caballero, fighting for the honor of the Pinzons he had always served.

Nell Brodie's voice dragged him back to the urgency of the moment. She was standing in the low doorway of the milk-house.

217

"Clem is all right again," she called happily. "Here he is, Mr. Banning!"

The young Cross Knife foreman came staggering out, gaze fastening on the burning ranch house. He was still in a daze—unable to comprehend what had happened. From the depths of the shadows made dense by the leaping flames rode Cordero's two vaquero recruits. Following them was a stocky, middle-aged rider, swarthy and fierce-eyed. A Yaqui, Banning saw. Three good men, he sized them up to be. With Cordero and these men—and the Devil's Bridge short cut—there was a chance—just a chance. And there was Brice—if he could get word to him. What were cattle—when Anita Callahan's safety was in the balance? He attacked the problem of Brice furiously. Clem Sanders was the only man there, excepting himself—who knew Brice. It was Clem's job to find the Broken Ladder man down there in the maze of canyons where Stenger and his gang were making ready for the drive to Lobo Pass.

Wordlessly the little group watched him as the thoughts tumbled through his mind. Clem Sanders broke the silence.

"The hell hounds!" His voice shook with fury—with dawning comprehension of what that burning house portended. "The hell hounds!" His distraught gaze went to the girl by his side. "Nell! What am I standing here for? What are we waitin' for—when they're doin' this to you?" He took a quick step from the doorway. Banning saw that realization had sent a new tide of vigor surging through the stocky young body of the Cross Knife foreman.

"Feeling fit to ride again, Clem?" he queried.

"Fit to ride to hell—if it's to get them devils!" Clem answered wildly.

"Listen." Banning drew the younger man aside and in a voice inaudible to Nell, briefly told him of her father's murder.

"You are all she's got now, Clem," he told Sanders. "You—and Anita Callahan. And Anita—she's in one bad fix. We're needing help—and you're ridin' to get it for us."

Sanders listened coolly while Banning explained the situation. "Brice and his men will be down in one of those brush canyons north of the Little Anita," he told Sanders. "Was planning to surprise 'em on three sides as they pushed into Little Anita Canyon. Brice knows you—will take your word for it that we're needing him in a hurry at the Cross Knife. Tell him to forget the Stenger gang and come on the jump with his rannihans." Banning paused. "Too bad about those Box B cattle," he added. "Reckon we'll pick 'em up later."

"I'm drawin' Anita Callahan's pay," Sanders said with stiff lips. "I'm still workin' for the Cross Knife, Banning. Anita's got first call on me—but when this shindig is done—" He glanced at Nell Brodie—"there'll be just one girl I'm workin' and fightin' for." The young cowman's face hardened. "There's two things has me worried. I'm needin' a gun—and this Devil's Bridge short cut has me up in the air. Ain't never heard of it."

"Cordero," called Banning. "Any of these men here know the Devil's Bridge short cut?"

"Him know." Cordero jerked a thumb at the fierce-eyed Yaqui. "Him old Cross Knife man."

"Clem is riding for help," Banning told him. "The Yaqui must go with him—act as guide. Clem don't know this Devil's Bridge short cut and I reckon none of the Brice outfit will know." Banning's hands went to his empty holsters. "Got any extra guns with you, Cordero?"

"*Si*—your own guns, Señor," returned the old man. He went to his heavy, silver-mounted saddle and produced the black-handled guns from a leather pocket. "I see them throw guns in brush when you made preesnor."

Banning snatched them with a delighted grunt —thrust one into his belt and handed the other to Sanders. "Shoots the same shells you've got in your belt, Clem. All right—let's ride."

"But Nell?" Sanders' voice was panicky. "Can't leave her here alone!"

"She's coming with us," said Banning. "Nothing else she can do."

Sanders nodded and went swiftly to the girl. "I've some business down in the canyon," he told her. "Banning says you're to ride to the Cross Knife with them." He kissed her startled, upturned face and turned away. She hastened to overtake him.

"I'm going with you!" she declared resolutely. He started to protest. Nell's eyes flashed. "No use arguing about it, Clem Sanders. I'm going with you—or I'll stay here—alone."

"She's right, Clem," broke in Banning. He gave the girl an admiring smile. "Reckon it's for her to say what she wants to do." He swung into his own saddle. "Let's ride," he told Cordero.

Cordero was addressing the Yaqui in Spanish. The man nodded, swung his horse and followed Clem and the girl, already on the run for their horses.

As they rode out of the yard, a rifle cracked somewhere in the distance. Tensely, Banning listened. Again the roar of a rifle, followed quickly by the lesser reports of six-guns. The fight in the Little Anita was on. No chance for help from Brice now. Banning gave Cordero a haggard look.

They tore into the misty moonlight of the rolling uplands, pressing toward the sentinel spire of El Toro. Behind them the flames from the burning ranch house became a crimson glare in the night sky. Below—in the dark canyons of the

221

Little Anita, like serpent's darting tongues, spat vicious red streaks as the Broken Ladder men battled with the rustlers.

Cordero's speedy Palomina set a fast and furious pace. Not once did the old man falter, twisting and turning through mesquite and cactus with scornful disregard of lack of trail. Gaspar Cordero's years in the Spanish Sinks had been too many for him to need a beaten trail to follow. Like a swift-flying eagle he made his swoop for Devil's Bridge—the short cut to the Cross Knife Rancho.

It was well named, Banning saw. A great arch of granite, reaching over a narrow gorge from sheer wall to sheer wall, with the confined waters of the Big Anita roaring turbulently five hundred feet below. A slippery, perilous bridge, rounded at the top and less than ten feet wide. A single misstep —a dizzying plunge—and death on the foam-flecked rocks half a thousand feet down.

The Palomina took it without a falter. The big stallion followed next, steady under Banning's reassuring hand. Felipe Mandoza's roan pressed closely after—gained across. They turned to watch Ramon, now descending the arch. The horse halted, ears flattening in terror. They saw briefly the rider's face, greenish gray in the moonlight as horse and man slid off into space. A wild, despairing scream—the rest was lost in the titanic thunder of the Big Anita.

The appalling suddenness of it left Banning and Felipe white and shaken. Of the three, Gaspar Cordero alone retained his imperturbable calm. He had seen death too many times.

"Come," he said, "it ees not far now—to the hacienda." He gestured for Banning to look.

Less than a mile distant spread the rich pasture lands of the Cross Knife—the old walls of the ranch house showing gray through the shadowing trees.

Chapter XXII

Anita's momentary panic as she recognized the tall figure of Sassoon in the patio disturbed her. The sickening wave of fear left her limp—unnerved. It was absurd, she told herself angrily. Sassoon was Heaven-sent in this time of peril and need. His unexpected appearance should have sent relief surging through her—not this unaccountable alarm. Sassoon was, next to Asa Coons, the most powerful person in the Spanish Sinks. This last outrageous visitation from the King Buzzard—this threat at herself—would arouse him to action. He would surround her with protection.

Yet behind the maze of bolstering thought, Anita was secretly aware of an odd dismay that it was not Cal Banning hurrying to her across the moon-drenched patio.

Sassoon's voice reached her, agitated, apprehensive.

"You're alone, Anita?"

He came swiftly up the worn stone steps, glance roving past her down the length of the wide hall.

"Too much alone," she answered a bit hysterically.

"Was afraid you would be," Sassoon said.

"Heard that your vaqueros were on the run for the border. Knew what that meant." He eyed her keenly. "You're as white as chalk, Anita."

"Why shouldn't I be?" she flung back at him. "Coming home—finding the place deserted!" She swung into the hall, gestured at her portrait. "And finding *that!*"

Sassoon gave the black feather a moody glance. "Where is Clem Sanders?" he wanted to know. "Mean to say he's scared out—too?"

The whereabouts of her foreman was a mystery, Anita told him. "I'm terribly afraid that something has happened to him," she said. "Clem is not the kind to run away."

Sassoon's gaze fastened on the gun in her belt. "What's the good of that?" He gestured scornfully at the weapon. "Planning a fight?"

Anita resented the derision in his voice. "If you were the King Buzzard—you'd find out what I would do with it," she informed him furiously.

"Don't be childish," snapped Sassoon. "I was only joking."

"I suppose my nerves are on edge," confessed Anita. "At that," she added resentfully, "it's a poor time to joke."

"The ranch is no place for you to stay," he worried. "Anita—you must let me take you away —anywhere you like—outside of the Spanish Sinks." He looked meaningly at the black feather curled across the painted cheek of her portrait.

"You're in danger here—until we can clean out this gang of killers."

"I don't understand what it is all about," said the girl wearily. "What is it the King Buzzard wants? He has run off all the cattle—murdered poor Don Mike! What can he want with me?"

"Can't you guess?" Sassoon gave her a surprised look. "For one thing—he suspects you will never give up the fight to have him caught and hanged—"

"He's right in that belief," confirmed the girl fiercely.

Sassoon studied her thoughtfully. "There's a peculiar fact about these raids and killings," he continued; "they all seem to connect with water rights. Every rancher who has been driven away—or killed—owned valuable water rights. The Cross Knife controls the overflow from the Big Anita—practically the entire water-shed of the San Dimas. They got Don Mike because he refused to clear out. They've just burned out that homesteader, Kettler—want the big artesian well he brought in. And now—poor old Jim Brodie down on the Little Anita—"

Anita's horrified look stopped him.

"Jim Brodie—dead?" she cried.

"Brodie was killed this afternoon," he told her. "You didn't know?"

She shook her head. "Was it—was it—the King Buzzard?"

"Indirectly it was," said Sassoon. "Brodie rode into town with the news that he had been handed the black feather—warned to leave the country. He ran into Al Stenger—accused Al of being the King Buzzard. There was gunplay. Stenger claims he had to kill Brodie in self-defense."

"Jim Brodie was right," declared Anita. "Stenger is the King Buzzard—"

"You forget that Al Stenger happens to be my partner," reminded Sassoon coldly. "Surely you don't think I could be an associate of the King Buzzard?"

"Why—why—of course not," stammered the girl, flushed and uncomfortable under his reproachful smile. "He seems such an awful creature!" she burst out defensively. "I never could understand how you can abide him—be his partner!"

"Asa Coons could explain why," said Sassoon.

"Yes—I know how it happened," she admitted hurriedly. "Of course—there was nothing else you could do. It was take an interest in the Double S—or sell him out—ruin him—" She gave him a penitent look. "Asa Coons told me how you have tried to help Al Stenger—refused to foreclose the mortgage you held on his ranch." She paused, thoughts reverting to her own astonishing interview with the San Carlos banker. She told Sassoon of the mortgage held by Asa Coons—his offer to give her fifty thousand dollars and take the Cross Knife in settlement of Don Mike's debt.

"Seems like a good way out for you," commented the gambler. "It would be up to Asa Coons to handle the King Buzzard. He would do it—if he had to call in the United States Army for the job."

"Perhaps I would consider the offer—but for one thing," Anita mused. "It's that note Mr. Coons showed me," she told Sassoon. "I'm sure it is a forgery." She explained about the unusual omission in Don Mike's signature. "Grandfather always used the *Pinzon* when he signed checks and other business papers," she said positively.

"Doesn't sound like Ace Coons," demurred Sassoon. "He's one of the squarest men in the world. It's unthinkable!" he declared. "Don Mike was undoubtedly nervous—upset—over conditions forcing him to borrow money. He simply forgot—was careless."

"It was second nature for him to always sign his name in full," insisted Anita. "I've seen hundreds and hundreds of his signatures." Her eyes sparkled. "You can't make me believe that grandfather was so terrified he couldn't remember his own name. Don Mike never knew the meaning of fear."

"For once he did." Sassoon's tone was grim. "He knew what that black feather meant. And now—the same warning has come to you. Anita

—you must let me take you away from this dangerous place."

"I won't be taken away," she said stubbornly. She looked at him, suddenly remorseful for her lack of hospitality. She had never seen Sassoon so harassed—so completely done up. "You look horribly tired," she told him. "I'm going to get you a glass of wine—"

She needn't trouble, Sassoon answered abstractedly. He wasn't in the least hungry, he said. He appeared to be listening.

"What is it?" Anita was suddenly nervous again. "I—I thought I heard something—a footstep—"

"One of my men," Sassoon explained. "I told them to keep a watch on the house."

"Sounded like a window—somebody was opening a window," insisted the girl.

"One of the front windows was open," he told her. "I told Chico to close it. That must have been the noise we heard." He sat down on the settee under her portrait. "Let's sit here. I've something to tell you, Anita."

She obeyed, vaguely uneasy under his look. Sassoon had always been so impersonal with her—impersonal to the point of indifference. The expression now in his eyes was something she had never seen there before. Again that strange, unaccountable fear possessed her.

"About this note," Sassoon continued. "I've been thinking of a way out for you—" He paused, dark eyes burning—"Anita—I've been mad about you for months. Marry me—immediately. I'll settle this matter with Asa Coons—save the Cross Knife for you. Between Coons and myself—we'll run these King Buzzard killers out of the country—" His hand closed over hers—held it tight. "It would please Don Mike—and I know how to love a woman!" He leaned close, smiling into her startled, upturned face, his black eyes hot with suddenly unleashed passion.

Her speechless amazement seemed to anger him. She felt his arm slip to her waist, hard, unbreakable, pressing her slim body against him.

"Why not?" he demanded fiercely. "My blood is like your own—good Spanish blood. But for the Irishman—Michael Callahan—my great-grandfather would have become the husband of your great-grandmother." He gestured at the lovely face glowing from the wall. "He would have been the lord of the Cross Knife Rancho! It is not too fantastic that I should at least rule where my great-grandfather, Pablo Garcia, might have ruled. And I am wild about you, Anita! Wild to have you for my own. It will be the solution of all your troubles. The end of the King Buzzard."

Anita said faintly. "You're hurting me—please—Mr. Sassoon."

"Not Sassoon," he told her with a laugh. "I took the name when I came here—to be near the Cross

Knife—and you—hoping some day to realize the dream of my great-grandfather. "I am a Garcia—Pablo Garcia—and I've loved you ever since the first day I saw you, *Anita mia*! In you I saw my dreams fulfilled!"

"You're hurting me," she repeated, frightened. "Please take your arm away. It's all so—so strange. I must think."

His arm relaxed. She strained from him, golden brown eyes studying him with a mixture of scorn and curiosity.

"So—you want to marry me—for the Cross Knife?"

"The two overwhelming desires of my heart are the Cross Knife—and you," said Sassoon. He smiled. "Asa Coons' offer for the ranch was made in my behalf."

"That would mean fifty thousand dollars out of your pocket," she reminded cuttingly. "Marrying the owner is much cheaper." She shook her head. "Thank you for the doubtful compliment, Mr. Sassoon—or must I call you Mr. Garcia? If the worst came to the worst—I'm quite sure I would prefer to take the fifty thousand and let the love go."

"I'll have both," the man assured her. "You will never get away from me—now."

His confidence frightened her. "Are you—are you threatening me?" Her voice was unsteady.

"What else is there for you to do?" he

demanded. "You can't oppose the King Buzzard! I can save you."

Anita gave him a long look. "Are you the—the King Buzzard?" she asked quietly.

He parried the thrust good-naturedly. "There you go again. First it was Al Stenger. Now you accuse me." He laughed harshly.

"You talk so glibly about him," she said. "And just a moment ago—you told me it would be the end of the King Buzzard—*if I married you.*"

"I have my reasons for that statement." Sassoon's voice was like the purring of a great cat; his eyes glittered; he leaned toward her. "My dear Anita—what if I told you that I have cut the King Buzzard's wings—that before morning he will be dangling at the end of a rope—his gang scattered forever?"

"You mean it?" Anita sat up, electrified.

"Would you marry me?"

"Oh, please—don't keep me in suspense!" For no apparent reason she found herself thinking of Cal Banning with an insistence that left her giddy with longing to see him. "How do I know—now—what I would do?" she said faintly. "Can't we let all that work out as it will?"

"I've had my suspicions for some time," went on Sassoon, or Garcia, as he called himself. He paused, teeth gleaming white under the trim black mustache. "Stenger and I have trapped him, my dear. The reign of terror is over."

Anita's nervous gesture interrupted him. "I'm sure I heard something move—in there!" she whispered. She pointed at the portieres shutting off the drawing-room from the hall.

"One of my men," reassured Sassoon. He gave her a grim, twisted smile. "I told you I'd placed guards—"

"Sounded like someone in the room," she insisted.

Sassoon said impatiently, "I was telling you that we have the King Buzzard where he won't bother you—or anyone else ever again."

Instinctively Anita shivered under the man's gloating smile.

"This mean anything to you?" he asked. He fumbled a crumpled piece of paper from a pocket, smoothed it out and held it up to her gaze.

"Why—why—" The girl's face was suddenly ghastly. "It's—it's Cal Banning!" She stared with stunned, disbelieving eyes at the picture of the man wanted by the sheriff of Cochise. She felt she could scream.

Sassoon was speaking. His voice seemed miles away. "Cal Banning—wanted dead or alive—for cattle-stealing—murder—"

"I—I can't believe it!" she heard her own voice protest. "Cal Banning is not all those—those terrible things! He couldn't be!" Her horror-stricken gaze went to the heavy portiere across the hall—was vaguely aware that they moved slightly—as if billowed by a stirring of night wind from an open window. She was too paralyzed by Sassoon's disclosure to more than casually notice. She was in a daze—could think of nothing—only that Cal Banning was a hunted criminal—a murderer.

"More than all those terrible things," continued the purring voice of the man by her side, "he is the mysterious unknown terror of the Spanish Sinks."

"You mean—" She looked at him piteously. "No! Not *that!*"

"Absolutely that," said Sassoon in a harsh voice. "This man—Cal Banning—is the *King Buzzard*. Why—" He stopped, suddenly furious at the agony in her eyes. "What is he to you—that you need be so shocked? You ought to be glad that we've caught him—broken up the gang!"

"Yes," she said dully. "I—I was talking to him—only this afternoon—" She paused, achingly conscious of a growing and bitter rage. How gullible she had been! She had been ready to put her entire trust in this Cal Banning—had allowed him to convince her with his glib talk of working secretly with old Gaspar Cordero to disclose the identity of the King Buzzard. And all the time he was actually planning another diabolical crime—herself the unsuspecting victim! Cal Banning—the King Buzzard! Cal Banning—the murderer of Don Mike!

"He told me he was himself on the trail of the King Buzzard," she said in a hollow voice. "He was to be here—tonight—was going to work for me—"

Sassoon's smile was almost sinister. "He has handed out his last black feather," he assured her.

"I don't understand why you didn't tell me the moment you got here," complained Anita. "You saw how frightened I was—and yet you—you—"

His hand closed over hers, held it tight. "Perhaps I was trying to make you realize how dependent you were on my help," he said softly. Again his arm circled her waist, tenderly—almost humbly. "Anita—won't you admit now that I am of use to you—that you can come to love me?"

She wanted to cry out that she hated him—that his nearness—his touch—sickened her. The thought of Cal Banning crushed the impulse. She wanted to hurt Cal Banning. If marrying Sassoon could add to his punishment—why—it would not be so hard to marry Sassoon. She would do anything—*anything*—if it would add to the hell waiting for the man who had killed Don Mike.

She sat stiffly, pliant body tense under the pressure of the encircling arm. She wanted to say something nice to this man—something that would give him hope—yet not be an absolute promise. The words refused to come. She tried to look at him—was unable to sustain the passion in the black eyes watching her so intently. His breath was hot on her white, strained face. She averted her eyes—stared blindly at the heavy portiere across the hall. Again it seemed to move—yet there was no stirring of air. She watched it apathetically.

"You don't need this now," Sassoon said in her ear. His fingers loosened the gun belt from her waist; it slid to the floor—lay at their feet. His other arm went suddenly around her; before she was aware of his intention, he was holding her helpless—his face bending down to her lips.

"No!" she exclaimed frantically. "No! Don't—I couldn't bear it!" Panting, panic-stricken, she struggled desperately to free herself. "I don't like you—never will like you!" she gasped.

Sassoon was panting, too, his face darkly-flushed.

"You little tiger-cat! You will kiss me—and like it!" he snarled.

"Not if the lady objects," said a chill voice.

Chapter XXIII

With a startled oath, Sassoon's gaze whipped round to the portieres—to the tall figure of Banning, framed between their wine-red folds. His arm fell away from the girl, his ardor gone from him like the air from a pricked toy balloon. Anita sprang to her feet.

"You!"

There was uncontrolled joy in her voice. Then she remembered. This man was the King Buzzard—the slayer of her grandfather; Sassoon had just told her so—shown her that terrible picture of a killer wanted by the sheriff of Cochise! The thoughts tore through her like searing bullets, racked her body, tortured her heart, left her shaken, trembling. She saw him as through a haze, tall, powerful body panther-taut, gray eyes in the keen hawk's face, watchful, unwinking—twin points of chilled steel as they clashed with the glaring, snarling gaze of the man huddled on the settee. And of a sudden Anita knew with every pulsing beat of her racing heart that Sassoon had lied. Cal Banning was not the King Buzzard—was not even a fugitive from the law. She took a step toward him.

"He said you are the King Buzzard!" she cried. "I know now that he lies—you are not the King

Buzzard! You don't even need to tell me you are not! I know—down in my heart I know—in spite of him!" Her dark eyes flamed round at Sassoon's ghastly, distorted face.

"No," said Banning slowly, "I am not the King Buzzard." His gun menaced the man on the settee. "Keep as you are, Sassoon. I don't miss—when I shoot to kill—and killing you—would not be murder." He moved his arm slightly, disclosing the star of a deputy United States marshal pinned to his shirt. "See that, Sassoon? That's my authority empowering me to arrest you alive—or dead." In a louder voice he added significantly, "Doc Spicer's Indian talked—before he died—talked to Gaspar Cordero—"

As if the words were a signal, the velvet hangings swished aside, revealing the old innkeeper's massive person. Anita stifled a gasp. She had never before seen Gaspar Cordero in the resplen-dent dress of the old Cross Knife days. He seemed years younger than the aged man she had known. Even the sunken eyes shadowed under the great sombrero seemed to burn with the live, hot flame of youth as they fastened on Sassoon.

"Tell the señorita who knifed the Indian," directed Banning.

"These man, Smoky Kile," said Cordero briefly.

Anita's eyes widened. "But who killed the doctor?" she queried, after a moment's stunned pause. "Not Smoky Kile that time—because he was in the room when Doc Spicer was shot—from outside." Her gaze went to Sassoon. "You!" she said accusingly. "*You*—were the only man—not there in that room."

"He sneaked over from the chapel," Banning told her. "Sassoon realized that Doc Spicer would talk—tell what he knew—and shot him in the back. Smoky Kile told the Indian before he knifed him—that Sassoon had done for the doctor."

Banning gave the girl a rueful smile. "Remember how we all went chasing into the garden—looking for the killer? Smoky Kile was afraid I'd spot Sassoon before he got back to the chapel, and whacked me on the head with his gun—tried to make me believe I'd run against a tree stump. It was pitch dark; I wasn't sure myself what had happened until I got a look at his gun later that night. Found hair and blood—smeared on the barrel."

Anita nodded. "I remember—that awful gash on your head—" Again she looked at the man cowering on the settee, horror growing in her eyes, and unutterable loathing. She understood, now, what had bred that unaccountable fear when she had recognized Sassoon coming toward her across the moonlit patio.

"You," she said in a stunned voice, "*you* are the King Buzzard!"

239

He gave her a terrible look—seemed to crumple under the charge.

"The jig's up," Banning told him grimly. "We've got you, Sassoon—and we've got a bunch of your men safely hog-tied out there in the corral. And something else you won't like—" Banning's voice was jubilant. "There's a herd of cattle heading into the Sinks, mister. Cross Knife cattle that our old friend, Windy Ben Allen found below the line on the Rancho Estero—the old Garcia hacienda—"

"That's his name," exclaimed Anita. "Did you know?"

"Knew the minute I saw him in the Horsehead Bar," grinned Banning. "Recognized him as Pablo Garcia the moment I laid eyes on him. The mystery began to unravel, then. I sent old Ben Allen across the line for a look-see."

For the first time, Sassoon spoke, his voice husky. "Damn you, Banning! What brought you into this?"

"Don Mike set the wheels in motion," the young deputy United States marshal told him grimly. "He'd been warned—the black feather—and sent word to old Bill Brice of the Broken Ladder. Brice took it up with a couple of other outfits— Jim Blair of the Frying Pan, and Norton of the Wagon Wheel. They figured I was the man for the job—fixed me up with this deputy marshal badge and sent me high-tailin' for the Sinks."

Banning grinned again. "The sheriff of Cochise was kind enough to fix me up with that piece of paper—makin' me eligible to join the King Buzzard's gang," he drawled.

"Damn you!" snarled Sassoon. "I know you—now!" He glared venomous hate. His glance shifted, fixed on the miniature of the first Don Mike Callahan. "I've always hated you Callahan men!"

"What does he mean?" demanded Anita, puzzled, and sensing an extraordinary revelation.

"The señorita has not suspec'?" Gaspar spoke softly, a curious smile on his granite face. "These yong man—he ees a Callahan, my señorita."

Anita gasped, golden brown eyes fixed wonderingly on the tall deputy marshal. Slowly she turned and gazed at the portrait of old Don Mike.

Cordero nodded. "I theenk you onderstan', no?" he murmured.

She shook her head. "No—I don't understand—quite—" She looked at Banning. "It is very strange! I was looking at that picture of grandfather—this evening—thinking you resembled him—the hair—the eyes—but not the nose. Your nose is higher—sort of Indian—"

"Hees gran'father was twin broder of Don Mike," cut in old Gaspar. He darted a savage glance at Sassoon. "These man's great-gran'father lofe the señorita Anita Pinzon before she marry with your great-gran'father. He ver' angree when she choose the yong gringo for husban'. These Garcia hombre want revenge, an' when these twins born he steal one twin—take heem to Mexico an' give heem to Yaquis. The boy take Yaqui chief's girl for hees wife an' run away to Texas." Cordero's eyes twinkled. "These Yaqui girl hees gran'moder—" He nodded at Banning. "She give heem those nose."

"It's the strangest story!" marveled the girl. She drew in a long, contented breath. "A wonderful story," she added, giving Banning a shining-eyed look. "So—so I'm not the last of the Callahans after all!"

"I'm a Callahan," he assured her. "Michael Banning Callahan." His gray eyes smiled at her. "Back at the Frying Pan—where I was foreman— they called me plain *Mike*—"

"No, Señor—you are the yong Don Mike," grunted the old ex-majordomo of the Cross Knife.

Anita blushed furiously. "The cattle!" she exclaimed hurriedly. "Is it true—really true—that you have found them?"

"Reckon they're in Lobo Pass by this time," answered Michael Banning Callahan. "Soon as old Windy Ben brought the news, the boys from the Frying Pan and the Wagon Wheel high-tailed it for the Rancho Estero to round 'em up. Jim Blair of the Frying Pan has good friends in Mexico. There'd be no trouble fixin' things with the government." He grinned at Pablo Garcia, alias Joe Sassoon. "Stenger was right, mister. The King Buzzard has pulled off his last raid." His voice hardened. "Cordero—search that man for a gun. Usually carries a shoulder-gun under his coat."

"*Si*, Señor," grunted Cordero. He took a step from the red hangings, halted as Sassoon slid limply from the settee.

"Look out!"

The deputy marshal's warning cry was too late. Startled by the limp body crumpling near her feet, Anita shrank directly in front of the officer's gun. Before he could shift the weapon, Garcia had the gun from Anita's holster lying on the floor—was pointing it straight at the petrified girl.

"Drop your gun, Callahan!" he snarled. "You, too, Cordero—or the girl dies!"

There was a silence—then the thud of guns on the thick rug.

"You carry two guns, Callahan," reminded the gambler. "Get rid of it—no tricks—if this girl's life means a thing to you."

"Haven't got it with me," replied the young deputy marshal. His face was white. "Gave it to Clem Sanders—"

Keeping the six-shooter pressed against the girl's back, Sassoon, or Garcia, to give him his true name, cautiously got to his feet, free hand slipping the shoulder-gun from under his coat.

With the second weapon, he covered the two men.

"An error on your part, mister—not to have 'hog-tied' me as you say you did my men," he sneered. "Also—" He laughed mockingly—"let me inform you that I am not the King Buzzard." His laugh came again, mirthless, sinister. "The King Buzzard is about due—in fact I am sure he is very close—"

From somewhere outside came the unmistakable clatter of hoofs. Garcia smiled, motioned to Anita. "Nearer the door, my dear. As soon as I have settled accounts with your friends—we will ride south—you and I—back to the land of our own people."

She obeyed, white-lipped, dumb with terror. Callahan spoke quietly.

"Garcia—you haven't a chance to get away. You'll find Lobo Pass choked with Cross Knife steers—and with them half a hundred armed men."

"I think I mentioned something about the King Buzzard," reminded the man. "He'll be riding with me, Callahan. We'll pick up those steers and take them along with us. Naturally we'll be leaving the Spanish Sinks for good. At least you triumph there, Callahan—but you won't live to enjoy the triumph." He paused, listened. The night seemed to throb to the pounding thud of galloping hoofs. Garcia resumed his low, cat-like purring.

"You'd never guess who is the King Buzzard,

Callahan. I'm the only man who has seen his face. Remember that night in San Carlos? When the mysterious black-cloaked horseman rode down the street and left his calling cards on me and Coons? That was the King Buzzard, Callahan. A black smoke in the night, Chico told us. Ha! A great man—this King Buzzard. But for your meddling—we would have owned the entire Sinks—with myself lord of the Cross Knife hacienda—" Garcia broke off, startled, surprised face half turned toward the door. Again came the unmistakable bark of a six-gun—followed by the scream of a wounded man—and suddenly the night air shook to the crashing roar of fast-working six-shooters.

"Brice!" yelled the deputy marshal. "It's Bill Brice and his Broken Ladder boys—at grips with the gang!"

Garcia's gun menaced him. There was an insane glare in the man's black eyes. "Won't help you, Callahan. Keep those hands up!" He backed toward the door, pausing near the girl.

"No chance for you to get away now, Garcia," Callahan told him coolly. "Don't make bad matters worse. They'll be bound to get you."

"I'm getting you first, damn you—" Snarling-lipped, Garcia lifted his gun. There was a scream from Anita—a flash of gleaming steel from the dark interior behind the wine-red portiere—Garcia staggered—gave a queer bubbling gasp—

sank to his knees and toppled over on his side, gun exploding harmlessly.

Callahan made a swoop for his black-handled gun—sprang to the fallen man. Transfixed in Garcia's throat was a long-bladed knife.

"What happened?" Anita tottered toward the deputy marshal. "Oh, Cal—I thought the—the end had come!"

"He's dead—Garcia's dead," he told her. He put an arm about her—looked gratefully at the lithe young vaquero framed between the portieres.

Felipe Mendoza grinned. "The knife ees more better than the gun—sometime, Señor," he said with a deprecating shrug.

Above the crack of six-guns, the shrill yells of fighting men, came the sound of booted feet clattering across the patio stones. The deputy marshal pushed the girl to one side gently and sprang to the door, followed by Cordero and Felipe, guns drawn.

"It's Brice," exclaimed the young man in a relieved voice. "And old Ben Allen." He looked round at Anita. "Clem is with them—and Nell Brodie!"

With a joyful cry, Anita darted past him into the moonlit corridor. "Nell!" Her arms went around the weary girl clinging to Clem Sanders.

"We've got 'em on the run," Brice tersely told Callahan. He grinned. "Got the Stenger bunch, too. Man—it was a massacre. They didn't know what was happenin' to 'em."

"Good work!" The young deputy marshal grinned. "Sure glad you got here, old timer. Some ride, huh—over that Devil's Bridge?"

"Lost a man there," Brice muttered. He glanced at Nell Brodie. "Clem wouldn't let the girl try it. Carried her across in his arms." Brice paused. "Heard shootin' over here—so we come runnin'—" He broke off, stared at the prone form lying inside the door. "Sassoon, huh?" He shrugged. "Reckon I'll get back to the boys. Come on, Ben—you old sidewinder."

Windy Ben grinned—tapped his huge six-shooter significantly. "I got Stenger," he informed Callahan. "I sure settled with him for old Jim Brodie." He swaggered off behind the tall Broken Ladder man.

The sound of conflict was drawing away from the ranch house. Callahan's gaze went to the still form of Pablo Garcia, alias Joe Sassoon, lying there inside the door. If this man was not the arch-criminal known as the King Buzzard—who was?

Suddenly the amazing answer came. With a stifled exclamation, the young deputy marshal went quickly into the hall, his eyes beckoning Cordero and Clem Sanders. Anita was moving down the corridor, comforting arm around the sobbing Nell Brodie.

"I'm riding," Callahan hurriedly told the men. "You fellows—and Felipe—stick close to the house and keep an eye on things. Brice says the gang is on the run—but no sense taking chances of anything happening to the girls." He went swiftly down the hall. "And get that dead man out of here," he called over his shoulder.

He jerked open the massive front door— vanished into the night.

Chapter XXIV

Swiftly the big bay stallion surged across the moon-drenched desert, dust spurting in a low, trailing banner from powerful pistoning heels.

From distant canyon and brush-clad hill faintly sounded diminishing bursts of gunfire as the Broken Ladder men relentlessly pursued the fleeing rustlers.

The stallion's rider knew that somewhere in front of him fled the gang's master mind—the scheming arch-fiend man called the King Buzzard —winging frantically through the night to the safety of the cunningly concealed nest that had so amazingly defied detection. Its camouflage was gone now—stripped clean in the twinkling of an eye. Young Callahan knew that each drumming hoof-beat under him was drawing him nearer the quarry.

The crack of six-guns no longer clamored from the hills. The brooding silence of the desert closed around him, the quick rhythmic thud of the stallion's iron hoofs tearing a narrow lane through the engulfing stillness. Clumps of ragged mesquite and bristling cactus floated past—weird, fantastic shapes—and indistinctly at first—and almost one with the shifting shadows, Callahan saw the black-cloaked horseman in front of him.

As if sensing victory, the stallion's stride lengthened in a burst of speed that seemed magically to pull the laboring black horse and its cloaked rider to close foreground. The deputy marshal could see the man distinctly now, humped monkey-like in the saddle, a curiously squat figure, cloaked with flowing black cape, wide-brimmed black hat pulled low over face.

Steadily the stallion's terrific pace cut down the distance. The black-cloaked figure glanced over his shoulder, spurts of flame lancing from his hand.

Beyond loosening his own gun, Callahan made no attempt to return the fire. He wanted to take this man alive. If he tried it again, though, the deputy marshal's gun would beat him to it. The bay stallion was too good for this foul killer's bullets.

The winding trail brought them abruptly to the silently flowing waters of the Big Anita, the ebon horse a scant fifty yards in the lead. Beyond them, reaching across the treacherous quick-sands of the stream, was the narrow gravel bank of Callahan's Crossing. Without attempting to slacken speed, the black-cloaked rider drove his horse furiously into the ford, showing like a rippling silver streak between the deeper, darker waters.

For a moment horse and man disappeared in a leaping cascade of glittering spray, the impact of

the water bringing the black to a rearing standstill. Before the animal could recover footing,
Callahan was less than ten yards from the bank.

There was a strangled cry from the black-
cloaked rider, and under the gouge of his spurs
the black horse surged madly away. The man
glanced back, gun lifting in hand. Callahan's
heavy .45 roared. The black horse screamed,
reared, plunging and ploughing from the gravel
bank into clutching quicksands that almost
instantly dragged down his great weight. There
was another strangled cry from the black-cloaked
rider as the unfortunate horse sank under him,
leaving him floundering helplessly some fifty feet
from the crossing where his pursuer had halted.

Silent now, he struggled impotently against the
clammy death that was quickly dragging him
down, arms flailing under the folds of his black
cape—like the sable wings of some monstrous
bird. The wide-brimmed hat slithered into the
water, and Callahan saw the long, flat, bald head,
the vulpine face, of Asa Coons, peering above the
dark water with eyes not hidden now behind
amber spectacles—eyes that saw him clearly
enough—eyes that were cesspools of wickedness.
No wonder Asa Coons had covered them from
the world.

There was nothing that Michael Callahan could
do—nothing he wanted to do. After all—it was a
fitting end for the King Buzzard—this execution

in the implacable sands of Callahan's Crossing.

Cautiously he faced the stallion round to the shore. When he looked again—only a few bubbles marked the spot where Asa Coons had been—and presently the bubbles, too, vanished—the river flowing smoothly agleam under the moon. . . .

The deputy marshal found Anita waiting up for him when he returned to the ranch house. It was impossible to think of sleep until she knew what had happened, she told him. Of course there had been only one explanation for his sudden disappearance. Gaspar Cordero and Clem Sanders had refused to admit anything. She had been dreadfully worried, she reproached. He might have run into a trap—anything might have happened to him.

Briefly he told her what had occurred at Callahan's Crossing.

"You know," said Anita, "I'm not so terribly surprised. After you left I had a curious feeling about it—it came to me that Asa Coons was the King Buzzard. I should have suspected something of the truth when he showed me that forged note. I forgot," she went on as he gave her a questioning look. "You don't know about the note. Asa Coons claimed he loaned grandfather two hundred thousand dollars on his note—with the cattle as security. He showed me the note; it wasn't signed the way Don Mike always signed his name. I should have known then—about Asa Coons."

"It's all over," young Callahan told her. "You can put it all behind you."

"All over," she agreed softly. "Oh, the feeling of it—to know that it *is* all done with—put forever out of our lives!"

As often the case when release comes from too great a burden, Anita was suddenly buoyantly merry. She seized his hand—dragged him to the portrait of old Don Mike.

"It's you," she laughed, "all but *the nose!*" She ran on, gleefully pointing out the resemblance. "It's marvelous," she said. "No mistaking that you're a Callahan!" She paused, smiled mischievously. "Oh, I've some wonderful news! I'll give you one guess." She went on, giving him no time to guess. "Nell Brodie and Clem are to be married a week from today in our chapel. I'm giving them a real wedding party—with all the people from all over. They're going to build a new house on the Box B and live happily ever after—like they do in the stories—"

The look in his eyes left her a bit dizzy—but not as dizzy as the look he read in hers left him. He went suddenly pale.

"Why not—why not *two* weddings—in the old chapel?" he said in a low voice.

For a long, revealing moment they looked at each other, both pale now. Anita nodded her dark little head, the delicate color waving into her cheeks.

"Why not?" she answered breathlessly.

They talked the foolish little nothings always so vastly interesting to young lovers. "I like your hair," Anita told him. The fingers of her little hand caressed his dark reddish thatch. "There are so many things I like about you," she declared. "In fact, Mister Deputy Marshal—I find you strangely fascinating."

"If I tried to tell all the things I like about you —I'd never finish the story," he told her. "There'll always be a new chapter—a more beautiful chapter—and I'd have trouble finding words worthy of you."

"You'll have a lifetime to tell me the story," Anita assured him. "I'll never tire of hearing you tell it to me." Her glowing face lifted to his. "My Don Mike," she said softly. "You are my dear Don Mike!"

Unnoticed by either of them, the wide patio door opened; Gaspar Cordero entered the hall with his usual soundless tread. He halted abruptly. For a long moment he stared down the hall. What he saw evidently pleased him enormously. He nodded, smiled, backed on noiseless feet into the corridor, and quietly closed the door.

Center Point Large Print
600 Brooks Road / PO Box 1
Thorndike ME 04986-0001 USA

(207) 568-3717

US & Canada:
1 800 929-9108
www.centerpointlargeprint.com